Lucky Little Things

Lucky Little Things

JANICE ERLBAUM

Farrar Straus Giroux · New York

Farrar Straus Giroux Books for Young Readers
An imprint of Macmillan Publishing Group, LLC
175 Fifth Avenue, New York, NY 10010

Printed in the United States of America by LSC Communications,
Harrisonburg, Virginia
Designed by Aimee Fleck
First edition, 2018
1 3 5 7 9 10 8 6 4 2

mackids.com

Library of Congress Cataloging-in-Publication Data

Names: Erlbaum, Janice, 1969- author.
Title: Lucky little things / by Janice Erlbaum.
Description: First edition. | New York : Farrar Straus Giroux, 2018. |
Summary: Eighth-grader Emma Macintyre is mourning the loss of her mother's best friend and struggling to keep her own friend from drifting away when she receives a mysterious letter telling her to list ten lucky things she would like to have happen.
Identifiers: LCCN 2017042320 | ISBN 9780374306526 (hardcover)
Subjects: | CYAC: Luck—Fiction. | Friendship—Fiction. | Mothers and daughters—Fiction. | Single-parent families—Fiction. | Middle schools—Fiction. | Schools—Fiction. | Grief—Fiction.
Classification: LCC PZ7.1.E752 Luc 2018 | DDC [Fic]—dc23
LC record available at https://lccn.loc.gov/2017042320

For Mom

Contents

One

MONDAY HAS NEVER BEEN MY LUCKY DAY.

Monday, April 18, looked like it would be unlucky as usual. I was woken up before the alarm by our dog, Penguin, who sneezed on my face, and as I was stumbling half-asleep to go wash off the dog snot, I remembered two awful things:

1. It was Monday.
2. Aunt Jenny was still dead.

Aunt Jenny wasn't my real aunt, but she had been my mom's best friend since college. She and Mom did everything together and talked to each other every day. When my father moved back to Colombia after I was born, Aunt Jenny moved in with Mom to help take care of me. She stayed for almost three years. She saw me learn to walk and talk. She was there for all my birthdays and milestones. I thought for sure she would be there at my eighth-grade graduation this coming June, but back in October she got diagnosed with breast cancer, and then she was in and out of the hospital for surgeries, and then six weeks ago she died.

Mom and I were doing our best to act normal, but we were both really sad. Even sadder was watching Mom try to hide how sad she was. But I knew she was just trying to protect me by acting like she was okay. Mom's group of friends all say, "Fake it till you make it." Which means, "If you keep pretending to smile, one day you won't have to pretend anymore."

It's weirdly quiet in the apartment whenever I get up before Mom does. It makes me feel like I'm the adult. I have my routine down pat, so I can stumble through it: wash (usually) and dress (always), check my phone while I eat my cereal, then take Penguin for a quick visit to the hydrant on the corner of Second Avenue. Penguin's a little guy, not much bigger than my backpack. Mom and I got him from Waggytail, a shelter, two years ago, so we don't know exactly how old he is or what breed he might be. We think he's part pug, part bulldog, part who-knows-what else. Some kind of dog that sneezes a lot.

I was putting on Penguin's leash when I saw a small white envelope lying on the kitchen floor. Someone must have slipped it under the front door. Fran, our building's superintendent, who takes care of the plumbing and garbage and stuff, sometimes slips notes under our door when she wants to let us know the exterminator is coming. Fran lives in an apartment on the first floor behind the stairs, and I'm supposed to go knock on her door if I'm home alone while Mom's out and there's an emergency. But this didn't look like a note from Fran.

I picked up the envelope and saw my name on it: EMMA MACINTYRE.

Nothing else. Just my name. Not my address, not a return address, not even a stamp. My name was typed, not handwritten, so there were no clues there. I stared at it, trying to think what it could be, but I couldn't come up with anything except the obvious: It was a mysterious letter. And it was addressed to me.

So I opened it. Inside was a folded note, with the dirty-white edges of what looked like a dollar bill sticking out from each side of it. I pulled out the bill, and it was a twenty.

Lucky me! I thought, then opened the note. The first two words were in capital letters.

LUCKY YOU!

I closed the note.

Ooooohhhhhkaaaaaay. That was weird. I wasn't used to opening mysterious notes and finding the exact thing I was just thinking. But I wasn't used to opening mysterious notes and finding twenty bucks either, and that worked out pretty well. So I reopened the note and read on.

Your luck has changed for the better.

This twenty-dollar bill is the first of many lucky little things that will happen to you over the next thirty days.

You will not know when these lucky things are coming. You may not recognize some of them when you see them. Some, like this money, will be obvious right away. Others will take time to reveal themselves.

This is not a hoax. This is real, and here's how you can prove it:

Write a list of ten lucky little things you want to happen. At the end of the thirty days, look at the list and see what your good luck has brought you.

One rule: Don't tell anybody! No human person must know about this letter, or it won't work.

That was it. No goodbye, no signature. There was nothing on the back of the letter, and nothing else in the envelope. There were only those words typed on a plain white sheet of paper, and the twenty-dollar bill in my hand.

My heart beat fast. *Calm down,* I told myself. It was probably just a prank. But who sends someone money as a prank? There had to be a rational explanation. I wanted to ask Mom if she knew anything about it, but she was still asleep. Also, the letter said that if I asked Mom—who was, by definition, a human person—the luck wouldn't work.

I stuffed the letter in my pocket and puzzled over it as I walked Penguin. Was it some kind of test? Maybe some secret society was testing me to see if I could keep my mouth shut. If I could, they'd let me into their club. Or maybe someone put a hidden camera in the kitchen, waiting for my dumb reaction so they could make a hilarious gif out of it. That would be a nightmare. Or was there, just maybe, some kind of actual wizard who could do actual magic? No. I was a little too old to believe in that Harry Potter stuff.

I took the letter out of my pocket and reread the first line. *Your luck has changed for the better.* It reminded me of a fortune cookie—good news, but vague. Like a horoscope. Mom doesn't believe in horoscopes, but Aunt Jenny did. She was always telling me what a Virgo I am. ("You're so organized! You're so thoughtful! You're such a Virgo!") Aunt Jenny was a Taurus with Cancer rising, which . . . *Ha-ha, Life. Cancer rising. We get it—you're hilarious.*

Write a list of ten lucky little things you want to happen. That was more specific, but still not specific enough. What did "little" mean? For that matter, what did "lucky" mean? In the horoscopes, "lucky" meant "when things worked out the way you wanted them to." I was definitely due for some of that.

You will not know when these lucky things are coming. That part was almost spooky. And then, at the end, *No human person.* That was a strange way to say it. Was there such a thing as a non-human person? Like the tooth fairy, or the Red Power Ranger? Or maybe it meant a supernatural being? Great. So if I came across any supernatural beings, I could feel free to tell them about this mysterious letter.

I wanted to believe what the letter said. I wanted to believe that my luck had changed and I could look forward to a month of twenty-dollar bills falling out of the trees and landing at my feet. But I didn't want to be a sucker.

"Penguin," I said, "you didn't send me this note, did you?"

Penguin looked at me, then went back to sniffing street garbage and sneezing.

"No, it couldn't be you. Your typing sucks."

✉

Mom was up by the time we got back. She makes her own hours doing personal tech support, mostly from home, so she can work whenever she wants. When I was younger, I wanted to have the same job when I grew up, until I realized how eye-meltingly boring it is.

Mom was in her bathrobe making green tea at the counter. "Bloop," she said.

"Bloop" is our all-purpose word for "Hello," "Goodbye," "I love you," and "Look, we are both here in the same room."

"Bloop," I replied.

I took Penguin's leash off and studied Mom's back as she fixed the tea. Did she write the letter and put it under the door? It had to be her. It was the most likely explanation. But why would she do that? It wasn't her style at all. If she wanted to give me twenty dollars, she wouldn't put it in an envelope and make a big deal out of it. Also, Mom was crap when it came to keeping secrets. When she and Aunt Jenny first found out about Aunt Jenny's tumor, they agreed not to tell me for a week or two until they knew more—but then Mom immediately broke down crying that night and confessed everything.

I got my bag and put on my coat and kissed Mom goodbye, thinking how lucky it would be if I could go more than ten seconds without thinking about Aunt Jenny.

✉

The lucky letter seemed to beckon from my book bag as I walked to school. I kept trying to understand its instructions. *Write a list of ten lucky little things you want to happen.*

I wished there were more details so I knew how it was supposed to work. Everybody knows that genies give you three wishes, and you aren't allowed to use one of your wishes to ask for ninety-nine more wishes, and genies can't bring dead people back or make people fall in love. But the lucky letter didn't promise to grant any wishes. It told me to make a list of things I wanted to happen, so I'd know at the end if my good luck had been real.

It was almost like making a Christmas list. I didn't want to ask for too much good luck, but I didn't want to ask for too little, either. What did I want my good luck to bring me? Could I put *I become a famous actress and writer* on the list? Or *Tyler Hoff falls in love with me and takes me to a castle in Spain*? Somehow that seemed like stretching it, since (a) Tyler Hoff was one of the most popular guys at school, (b) he barely ever looked at me, and (c) he was terrible at Spanish.

I decided to focus on things that were like twenty dollars: nice things, but nothing life changing. You know, #realisticgoals.

Once I decided to keep it small, it was easy. By the time I got to school, I'd made most of my list, so I sat down before first period and started writing it out. There were so many things I wanted to happen:

1. Mom gets me a new phone.
2. Get a speaking part in the spring play.
3. Dakota likes me and invites me to hang out at her house with everyone.
4. Make out with Tyler Hoff.
5. Make new friends.
6. Mom gets a boyfriend or a social life.
7. Go somewhere good this summer instead of Grandma's.
8. Mom forgets my upcoming dentist appointment.
9. Savvy stops being weird to me.

Okay. Not to go off on a tangent here, but number 9 on my list wasn't such a little thing.

Savvy (short for Savannah) had been my best friend since third grade, when we discovered our mutual love of ZhuZhu Pets and One Direction.

We used to spend hours at her apartment after school making "art" out of macaroni and paper plates, playing video games, and pretending we were secret agents and her cat was the enemy. One of our favorite things to do was to plan out the thirty-room mansion where we'd live with our boyfriends/husbands/dogs when we grew up, because of course we'd live together when we grew up. We wore the friendship bracelets we made in the summer after fourth grade until they were raggedy gray strings on our wrists.

This was the year they broke.

In the fall, right around the time Aunt Jenny was diagnosed with cancer, Savvy's moms got her a real phone, and that was basically the end of normal, fun Savvy. Texting, Instagramming, and Snapchatting became her whole life. She started chatting with Dakota and the popular people, then she was hanging out with them on the sidewalk before class, and then she started getting invited over to Dakota's after school. Without me.

To be fair, I hadn't been around much this year, and when I was around, I was freaking out over Aunt Jenny. Savvy tried to be a good friend—she sent me funny animal videos and ridiculous jokes; she took me shopping at H&M and spent her entire Christmas gift certificate on me. One day I was crying, and she started crying, too, because she felt so sad for me. She even sent a card in the mail to Aunt Jenny, which made Mom and Aunt Jenny really happy. (I think Savvy's moms probably told her to send the card, but whatever. She did it.)

But since the funeral, she'd been acting strangely, almost avoiding me at times. She still sat with me at lunch, but now we sat at the table next to the popular crowd's, so she could turn around and join in their conversation, if they allowed it. I just wanted to spend an afternoon at Savvy's like we used to, before everything bad happened: watching random stuff online, making bizarre snacks from whatever was lying around her kitchen, discussing my love for Tyler Hoff and her love for whichever YouTube celebrity she was into that week. I wanted it to be normal with us again.

Having my friendship with Savvy back was the most important "lucky little thing" on my list. But I still had space for one more.

I thought about Mom. What about something lucky for her? The boyfriend and social life I wanted her to have were mostly for me, so she'd stay off my back. But what would be lucky for Mom? What did she want *her* good luck to bring? Maybe she could get a rich new client, one who paid in advance and then fell off a mountain in Tibet. Or maybe she could win a vacation to go snorkeling in Puerto Rico, like the trip she took before I came along, with Aunt Jenny and their friends Brik and Derek.

But Mom didn't care about snorkeling in Puerto Rico—not without Aunt Jenny there. All Mom really wanted was to have her best friend back.

Item number 9 on my list was for me to get my best friend back. Mom deserved the same. I knew it was impossible, and definitely not little, but the whole mystery-letter thing was impossible anyway, so I went ahead and made it item number 10 on my luck list:

10. Bring Aunt Jenny back.

Two

IT WAS HARD NOT TO TALK ABOUT THE letter at school. It had warned me not to tell any human person, but the minute I saw Savvy after first period, I wanted to yell, *Look! Look at this crazy mystery letter I got! WTH do you think it means?* But Savvy was doing something phone-based with Dakota and Sierra by their lockers.

I went over and said hi. Dakota and Sierra ignored me and kept looking at their phones.

Savvy looked up from her phone and murmured, "Hey."

She was wearing her mom Charise's shirt, a soft, loose, low-necked tee that slid all over her shoulders. It looked effortlessly cool, and we'd been admiring it for years.

"Hey," I said. "Your mom let you wear the shirt."

Dakota and Sierra immediately looked up from their phones and laughed.

"Your mom 'let you' wear the shirt?" Dakota repeated.

"That's your mom's shirt?" asked Sierra. "No wonder it's so outdated."

Savvy looked at me in horror, and I felt instantly awful. Why did I say something about her mom's shirt? Why did I say anything at all? Why couldn't I just be normal for a change and not ruin things?

I shot Savvy a look that said *I'm sorry,* then hurried away before I made things worse.

All morning I was distracted. By lunchtime I was dying to say something to someone. But I had to keep my mouth shut, at least for a day or two, until I knew for sure the letter was fake. If it was real, it could be my one opportunity to improve my luck. And if there was even a teeny-tiny chance it might result in something good for me, I didn't want to blow it on a technicality.

I couldn't say anything about the letter, but I could say something about the twenty dollars.

I showed the bill to Savvy at the lunch table, where we sat within hearing distance of Dakota's group.

"Look what I found this morning," I said.

Savvy nodded, distracted by her phone. After being separated from her beloved for two whole periods, she had to catch up on the latest pictures of people who were sitting two feet away from her.

"You *found* that?" Lewis Goldstein, the most obnoxious of the popular kids, scoffed at me from the next table. "Where? Like, outside on the ground?"

Lewis was a troll. All he did was pick on people to try to get them mad (which, btw, is not that hard to do), and then he'd be like, "Oh, I was just joking, stop being so sensitive." If he were taller and more muscled, he'd probably have been a bully, but he was thin and wimpy, so he was stuck being a troll. What's funny was how, back in fifth and sixth grades, Lewis was always getting picked on by Dakota and Tyler and the people he was friends with now. I used to feel sorry for him then.

"Yeah," I said. "I found it right by my building." (Right *in* my building, actually, but Lewis didn't need to know that.)

He laughed. "You didn't find that. You stole it. To give to your single mom."

Backstory: A few days before, I'd said something in social studies about being raised by a single mom, and everybody thought that was a dumb thing to say, like I was the only kid who'd ever been raised without a dad or I was trying to make my life sound harder than it was. Since then, it had become a running joke. I kind of hoped Savvy wouldn't chuckle along with everyone else, but she did.

Now Tyler jumped in. "That's why you're

crawling in the gutter for nickels." He put on an old beggar voice. "Please, spare some change for me and my single mom!"

This girl Naturi said to Dakota, "Must be hard to be so poor that you think twenty dollars is, like, something you tell people about."

Dakota imitated me: "Wow, I have twenty dollars! I can buy a house for me and my single mom!"

And then, as though I were not sitting right next to her, Savvy wrinkled her nose and said to the group, "I try not to . . . pick up stuff off the ground? Because . . . ew?"

So then it was a free-for-all. And I was stuck there in the middle of it. If I got up and left, I'd be a baby who couldn't take a joke. If I sat there stone-faced, they'd know they were really upsetting me and they'd go even harder. I had to just sit there and smile while they laughed and called me "Little Orphan Emma" and "Welfare Queen."

All because I'd mentioned the twenty dollars.

The twenty dollars that was supposed to be a lucky thing. At that moment it didn't feel lucky at all.

You know what would be lucky? I thought. *If a meteor slammed through the side of the building and crushed everybody here except me.*

I held my breath and hoped for a second. No meteor.

The stupid letter was obviously fake.

✉

The rest of that Monday was like any other awful Monday. Nothing especially good or bad happened after lunch, except I got a better grade than I expected on my science test. But I didn't think that was related to the letter. I took the test before the weekend, and I really studied for a change.

After school, we all hung out on the sidewalk as usual. The younger kids, and even some kids in our class, still got picked up by a babysitter or a parent. The rest of us, the mature and independent types, liked to stand there and witness their shame before we moved along.

Everybody was either on their phone or looking at somebody else's phone. *Blah blah blah.* Gotta put up new pictures of themselves doing duckface and making peace signs. Savvy kept moving around on the sidewalk like she didn't want me to stand right next to her. I could tell she was waiting to be invited to Dakota's house, but Dakota was ignoring her. Naturi and Sierra started walking backward toward Third Avenue, impatient for Dakota to join them.

"Let's go already!" Naturi called.

"I'm coming!" Dakota finished whatever she was doing and turned to Savvy with a smile. "Bye."

Savvy looked like she'd been punched in the gut. "Bye," she said.

"Bye," I said, though nobody was talking to me.

Dakota walked away.

"Bye!" yelled Naturi from halfway down the block. "Have fun, you two!"

Savvy went back to her phone. She looked like she was going to cry. In the old days, I would have suggested that we go look at wigs and glittery makeup at the drugstore. With my twenty, I could have bought us both fake eyelashes with rhinestones on them. Now I didn't know what to say.

"What?" said Savvy, not looking up from her phone.

"What what?"

"What do you want?"

Was she still mad from this morning, when I said the thing about her mom's shirt? I didn't do it on purpose. Meanwhile, she'd purposely made fun of me in front of everyone today. I was the one who should have been mad.

"Um, to see if you want to do something?"

She scowled and turned away, still bent over her phone. "*Obviously*, I'm busy. You don't have to stand there looking over my shoulder."

"I wasn't looking over your shoulder," I said. Now I was on the brink of tears for the second time that day. "Why are you being like this?"

"I'm not being like anything," she said. "Whatever." She started walking away.

I felt like running after her and kicking her in the back of the knee. Instead I yelled at her, "BYE, SAVANNAH!"

She hates her full name. ☺

✉

I stopped at one of my favorite stores and did a little shopping on my own, so Mom was out at an Alcoholics Anonymous meeting by the time I got home. Mom's not an alcoholic—she used to be, before I was born. She quit drinking fifteen years ago, but for some reason she's still supposed to go to meetings.

I was relieved that Mom wasn't home yet. Whenever she can tell I'm upset, she starts digging to find out what's wrong, and I didn't want to talk to her about Savvy.

I wished I could talk to Aunt Jenny. Aunt Jenny and I had a policy that I could tell her anything and she wouldn't tell Mom (unless I told her I was going to smother Penguin or something crazy like that). I know for a fact that she kept her word—she always deleted my texts right away so Mom wouldn't see them, even by accident, and one night when I was supposed to be asleep, I heard Mom raise her voice to Aunt Jenny in the kitchen.

"You can't let her keep secrets from me!"

Aunt Jenny's reply was loud, too. "Yeah? Guess what—you're her mom. She's going to keep secrets from you. Better that somebody knows what she's up to."

I heard Mom bang her fist on the counter. "That somebody should be me!"

"Well, it can't be," said Aunt Jenny. "Deal with it."

Typical Aunt Jenny. She always fought for what she thought was right, and she was never afraid to say how she felt. I could hear her voice in my head so clearly, it felt impossible that I would never hear it again in real life.

Since I couldn't talk to her, I scrolled through some old texts of hers I had saved.

One from last year, when she was healthy, and I was stressing over a crush who didn't crush me back:

> Not him! He looks like a jerk. Soccer jersey, Yankees hat, AND a skateboard? All he needs is a hockey stick and a Frisbee.

One from October, when she was going from tests to appointments to more tests, and I had to confess to my mom that I'd stolen money from her purse:

> Hate to tell you this, but she probs already knows. Just tell her and get it over with! She'll be happy you were honest. Just be super sorry about it!

One from December, when she was on her second round of chemo and surgeries, and I was upset because Savvy was being weird:

Tell Savannah Bananah I have a pic of her crying like a b**** at the end of Toy Story 3.

The pic was attached: Me, Mom, and Savvy were in our living room. Penguin was sleeping between me and Mom on the couch, and Savvy was in the big orange chair making one of those crying faces where your whole lower lip turns inside out and your chin gets shiny with drool and snot. If I had my own Instagram, I would *so* post the pic and tag Savvy.

Everything was great back then. My friendship with Savvy was tight. We were best friends, practically sisters, and we were going to live together in our thirty-room mansion until we died at the age of one hundred. How did things get so complicated?

✉

Mom came home from her meeting and poked her head into my room. She looked frazzled and worn out. "Bloop. Bloopity bloop."

"Bloop bloop."

"I got you a black-and-white cookie from Zabar's."

"Yay." I hopped off my bed to go get it, with Penguin close behind me.

Mom usually came home with something sweet after she went to one of her AA meetings. She met her last two boyfriends through the AA group near our house, so now she doesn't like to go to that group anymore. Fortunately for her, there's like seventy different group meetings in the city, and fortunately for me, she always gets me a black-and-white cookie when she goes to the one near Zabar's.

Mom settled down at the laptop on the kitchen table, aka her command center, and passed the cookie my way. This was my chance to really examine her and see if she knew anything about the mystery letter.

"What's new?" Mom asked, scanning her email, only half paying attention. She certainly was acting like everything was normal, so I acted like that, too.

"Nothing. Got an A on the science test."

"That's great! Sounds like you've caught up on . . . everything."

"Everything" meant all the school I'd missed during Aunt Jenny's last weeks, when I was absent so much that the principal said I might not graduate eighth grade if I missed another day. Now I wasn't allowed to get sick or injured until June 23. If my appendix burst on the subway one morning, I'd have to suck it up and get to school for attendance. Then I could go to the nurse.

"Yeah." I needed to steer the conversation toward the subject on my mind. "Lucky."

Mom frowned at an email and started typing. "Not 'lucky.' You worked hard."

"Same difference."

"Mmmmmm," she said. *Typety type type type.* "Luck is when you don't deserve something but you get it anyway."

"I thought luck was when you get the things you want to happen."

I watched her slyly. *Things you want to happen* was how the letter put it. So if she wrote the letter, she'd know I was on to her. But she didn't respond at all—she just kept typing.

"Maybe I don't know what luck is," she said.

Mom didn't seem interested in talking. I heard her mutter the words "duck knocker," so I knew whatever she was dealing with was bad. She used to curse a lot, until I was three years old and I asked her, "Mommy, what is a duck knocker?" After she literally fell on the floor from laughing, she started using it as her go-to curse word.

Mom wasn't that good an actress. If she was playing mind games with me, she wouldn't have been able to act so normal. I retreated to my room and left her to her knocking ducks.

I spent most of the night thinking about who was behind the letter.

Someone from school? No, the writing didn't

sound like a kid. And a mystery letter wasn't the type of thing a kid would come up with. A letter was way too old-school. I could safely rule out people my age, whether they were friends or enemies or both.

Fran, our superintendent? I thought I'd heard her footsteps in the hall that morning. She was a logical suspect, since she always slipped notes under doors, except that theory made no sense. Fran wasn't really involved in my life. She hadn't even been around much lately. She used to drop by our apartment once in a while to flirt with Aunt Jenny, but Aunt Jenny hadn't been here in a while, so neither had Fran.

Did Grandma send the letter? Hah! Grandma doesn't even send birthday cards, much less mystery letters. Also, she's three hours away by train, so she couldn't have hand-delivered it overnight.

If I was still seven years old, I might have thought the letter came from my father, Eduardo. That's back when I still thought my father was a magical man who watched over me in secret. I dreamed that he would appear in my life one day, take me away, and make me the princess of some far-off land. Then when I was ten, Mom and I flew to Colombia so I could meet him, and I saw who he really was: a boring jerk who'd cheated on his wife with Mom and then left town.

The letter didn't come from Eduardo. Nothing ever came from him, and nothing would ever come from him. Fine with me.

I couldn't think of anybody else to suspect. Day 1 of my magical lucky month was over, and I was no closer to understanding who had delivered this letter to me, how, or (most important) why.

I wondered what the next twenty-nine days would bring.

Three

DAY 2 OF MY LUCKY MONTH, AND THINGS were already starting to change for the better.

It started as soon as I got to school that morning. Savvy came right over to me and hugged me like everything was normal. "Hey," she said. "Sorry I was a binch yesterday. Ooh, I like those earrings."

"Thanks," I said. *I comfort-shopped them after our argument yesterday, with the twenty dollars you made fun of me for.* I kept that thought to myself. It was messed up how off and on Savvy was acting with me, but it did bother me less when she was on.

"I finished my self-portrait," she said. "Want to see?"

Savvy had been taking an advanced painting workshop on Saturdays at an old, fancy artists' club in the Village. The class was for adults, but one of her moms had a friend at the club who saw Savvy's work and decided to make an exception. For the past few weeks, she'd been working on a self-portrait in oils. She showed me a close-up pic of it on her phone.

Savvy had painted her face in two separate halves. Both halves looked like her, but one half looked more like her mom Charise and the other half looked more like her mom Ava. The realness of the image was astounding, even though the colors were bizarre—yellows and violets and acid greens. The thick brushstrokes gave it an almost rippled texture. It was breathtaking.

Savvy pointed at a few gray droplets in the background. They could have been raindrops or tears or ghosts. "Those are my bio dad," she said.

"This is amazing," I said. "Seriously. This is so incredible."

"Thanks," she said. "Next we're doing landscapes. I'm not that psyched."

I noticed as we walked into school that Dakota didn't seem to be there yet, nor was she there at lunch. Savvy and I sat at our regular table, and she did not spend the entire time turning around on the bench to talk to the rest of that group for a change. I couldn't help wondering how much Dakota's absence had to do with Savvy being so normal with me.

That afternoon, our English teacher, Ms. Engel, reminded us about the auditions for the middle school play. This was where I was really hoping for some luck. I had been in the chorus the last two years, but this year I wanted a speaking part, any speaking part that would allow me to actually act. I wasn't aiming too high—I knew I'd never get a lead role, because I can't sing very well. (And yet I kept winding up in the chorus, singing.)

"This year's play is not a musical," Ms. Engel announced.

Naturi and some of the other good singers in the class pouted.

"One of our upper school students has written a play that was selected for a Young Writers Award," Ms. Engel continued. "In honor of that achievement, for our middle school spring play, we will be doing Melanie Lambright's *Umbilical*."

A murmur swept through the room.

"*Unbiblical*?" asked this kid Shane.

Lewis the Troll laughed at him.

"*Umbilical*," Ms. Engel corrected him. "Like the cord. Since it's a straight drama, there are no songs or monologues to learn in advance. You'll get scripts at the auditions on Friday and read from those." She stopped and smiled. "As you know, in the theater, we don't say 'Good luck.' We say 'Break a leg.' So, to those of you who want to audition, break a leg!"

Everyone else started making jokes about

casts, crutches, breaking each other's legs, and so on, but I sat silent in my seat, stunned by what had just happened: When Ms. Engel said "We don't say 'Good luck,'" she had looked directly at me.

✉

Instead of going straight to lunch that day, I decided to chat with Ms. Engel.

I dropped by her classroom. She was sitting at her desk grading papers.

"Ms. Macintyre," she said. "What can I do for you?"

Um, Ms. Engel, you didn't by any chance sneak into my apartment building and slip a letter under my front door promising me little bits of good luck for a month, did you? Even in my head that question sounded insane. Why would she do something like that? I wasn't even one of her favorite students.

I sat down at a nearby desk. "Could you explain why actors don't say 'Good luck'?" I asked.

Ms. Engel looked pleased by my interest. "Well, it's just a superstition, really. You don't want to jinx another actor. Do you know what a jinx is?"

I did. It was like, if your team was winning in basketball, you shouldn't shout, "We're gonna win!" or that would be jinxing it.

"I guess it means, if you say something good's going to happen, saying it out loud makes it not happen."

"That's the idea," Ms. Engel said. "Or if you say it out loud, the opposite thing will happen. In the theater, we say 'Break a leg' because the opposite of breaking your leg is having a great show."

So if someone told me I was going to have good luck all month, was that a jinx? Did it doom me to thirty days of bad luck instead? Suddenly I felt scared. Was I cursed now? Was the money cursed? Were the earrings I bought with the money cursed? I should have burned that letter the minute I saw it.

"Do you believe in jinxes?" I asked.

"No," said Ms. Engel. "And I'm not afraid of things like black cats or broken mirrors. I think people come up with superstitions to try to explain things we can't explain."

"Do you believe in luck?"

"I believe we make our own luck," she said.

It would be great if adults occasionally answered questions with actual answers, like yes or no, instead of with confusing sentences. "What do you mean?"

"I mean, you will never be in the right place at the right time unless you go looking for the right places. It's like the school raffle. You can't win the raffle if you don't buy a ticket."

I nodded. Our school, Knights Seminary, holds a fund-raising raffle every year, and all students from grades K–12 can enter. I didn't buy a ticket last year, when the prize was a five-hundred-dollar gift certificate at the bike store on Sixth Avenue. I was jealous of the kid who won, but I never even took a shot at winning. This year, I would buy a ticket. Maybe two.

Ms. Engel continued. "So you can't count on good things or bad things to happen because of some mysterious sign. You have to try to make good things happen."

Right. Exactly. That's what I wanted to do. But . . .

"How?" I asked. "How do you try to make good things happen?"

She smiled and picked up her grading pen. "By trying."

We were just going in circles now. I got up from the desk. "Thanks, Ms. Engel."

"You're very welcome," she said. She went back to her work, and I turned to leave. Just as I reached the door, she said, "Emma."

I turned back around. She gave me the same look she had given me in class, like she was trying to tell me something important but couldn't say it in words. Had my hunch about her been right? Was she about to confess that she was behind the letter?

She said, "Break a leg on Friday."

✉

After school that day I had my volunteer project. My school wants everybody to volunteer, so they work with charities to find jobs for kids, and we get extra credit for doing them. My volunteer project this semester was walking dogs for Waggytail, the rescue shelter where we got Penguin. I liked everything about it, except knowing that these lovable dogs didn't have people or homes to go to. I was especially sad for this sweet dachshund mutt named Lancelot—the vet at Waggytail said Lancelot had a cancerous tumor in his leg. Lancelot was going to have his leg removed, but even that might not save his life.

I hate cancer.

I walked to the bus stop by school to go uptown to Waggytail. I usually have to wait a while for a bus, but today one pulled up to the stop just as I got there, and the door opened right where I was standing, like the driver had stopped personally for me.

I boarded the bus. As usual, there were no seats, so I stood. But as soon as I grabbed a pole in front of a guy in a seat, the guy got up and walked away. There was no reason for him to get up—we weren't near the next stop yet—but he left the seat open. So I sat down.

There was no traffic. And there's *always* traffic.

When I got to Waggytail, the founder, Holly, was practically jumping for joy. She hugged me as soon as I came in and told me the good news.

"We got the money to expand Waggytail! I never thought the grant I applied for would come through, but we just got the official call! Think how many more dogs we'll be able to help! And all the lucky people who will get to find their forever friends!"

"That's great!"

I knew how hard Holly and the rest of the staff worked to help dogs like Penguin. Holly's eyes were filled with tears of joy. Everybody there was so happy, dogs and people alike. In between walking and cleaning cages, volunteers were doing a lot of dancing and whooping and throwing dog toys at each other.

When we were done for the afternoon, one of the older volunteers had some pizza delivered, and we all sat around with the pups. It was one of the best days I'd ever had at Waggytail.

I was about to leave when Holly stopped me. "Emma! I was so happy about the grant, I almost forgot to tell you. Lancelot is going to be okay! He lost his leg, but the vet says he's cancer-free now, and he should have a long, healthy life ahead of him."

WHAT?

I couldn't believe what Holly was saying. Lancelot was going to be okay?

"Really?" I could feel myself getting ready to cry. I hoped I would not bawl in front of the other volunteers, especially the two who were near my age. But if Lancelot was going to be okay, I didn't much care where I bawled or who saw me. All I cared about was that Lancelot was cancer-free.

Holly smiled and nodded. "Sir Lancelot should be back from the vet this weekend. But he won't be here long. I know we'll find somebody terrific to adopt him."

I left Waggytail dumbstruck by all the good luck that had happened there. Whether or not it had anything to do with the lucky letter, I was grateful for it. I definitely would have put *Lancelot recovers from cancer* on my luck list, but after seeing what cancer did to Aunt Jenny, I didn't think it was possible for Lancelot to recover.

Now I'd received a fantastic lucky little thing for free.

Things were definitely looking up.

✉

I was in a great mood when I got home. I wanted to tell Mom the good news about Lancelot, but she was talking to a client on her earpiece. I texted Savvy to see if she maybe wanted to come over or something, or if I could go over there.

I tapped out my message and sent it:

Sup bish.

Savvy's reply came right away:

Go away speddy.

My heart sank into my stomach. "Speddy," of course, is short for "special ed." Which is short for "You are too dumb to walk among us 'normal' humans and should be banished to a classroom far, far away."

I was surprised to see Savvy use that word, because her mom Ava was a legal advocate for people with disabilities. Savvy didn't dare use words like "crippled," "lame," or "retarded," even among friends—one time when I was over for dinner, Savvy called something retarded, and Ava hit the roof. "You keep talking that way," she threatened, "and I will fry you alive and eat you for dinner."

Another text came through:

Sry. That was Tyler being dumb.

Oh. So Savvy was hanging out with Tyler's crew, probably at Dakota's, even though Dakota was absent all day and supposed to be sick. Dakota's mom had probably let her take a day off from school to handle the agonizing stress of being superior to everyone else.

It hurt to know that Savvy was hanging out with the love of my life without me, but at least it meant that *Go away speddy* didn't come from her. There was some comfort in knowing that my best friend didn't think I was dumb and want me to go away. Instead, it was the boy I liked who thought I was dumb and wanted me to go away. Improvement, but not by much.

I imagined sitting so close to Tyler Hoff that he could steal my phone. If he did, I would die instantly, because he'd see all my texts to Savvy about how I was in love with him. I'd liked Tyler since sixth grade—I didn't even know why anymore. I guess because he was popular and hot and untouchable, and I was used to him being my crush.

More texts came through, one right after the other:

ur depressing & boring

u always have to kill the vibe

u cry all the time

u don't know when ur not wanted

go away

WOW. Extra, extra harsh. They disliked me so much, they had to tell me about it in detail. Each text felt like another blow to the gut, and there was no way to tell who was typing and sending them. Dakota, Sierra, Naturi, Tyler, Lewis—they could be brutal. It could even have been Savvy. She could say whatever she wanted and blame it on someone else later—*Sorry, Dakota took my phone.*

How was I supposed to respond?

I texted back:

LOL.

I added the "crying from laughing so hard" emoji. That was me. *Nope, not crying, just laughing so hard I'm in tears.*

I was on the verge of chucking my phone out

the window and watching it smash to bits on the pavement below. Maybe then Mom would get me a new one. No, half the reason she made me carry the cheap one was that I'd lost two phones in a row when I was younger. Smashing this one would only make her say, *See? You're not responsible enough for an expensive new phone.*

"Bloop?" Mom called from the kitchen. "You want to go for a walk?"

Penguin certainly did. He jumped around at our feet and woofed.

I didn't feel like going out, but I didn't feel like staying home and looking at my phone, either. "Okay," I said.

We got our coats on and headed out toward the park. Mom seemed to be in a decent mood for a change. I saw an opening: Maybe I could try making my own luck, as Ms. Engel said.

"Moop?" (Mom + bloop = Moop.) "Do we have to stay at Grandma's beach house all summer this year?"

Mom raised her eyebrows. "That's an interesting question."

I sighed. Again, it'd be great if adults could just give you a simple yes or no. But nothing was simple when it came to Grandma.

I only had one grandparent, Mom's mother. I'd never met my father's parents, and Mom's dad died before I was born. But my one grandma was more than enough. Maybe even too much.

I shouldn't say that. Grandma means well, and she pays for my tuition every year. But Grandma likes to drink cocktails, which is hard for my mom to deal with, what with her own past problems with alcohol. After two or three cocktails, Grandma gets really cranky and critical of everything. I was tired of hearing about my "dusky coloring," my "wide frame," and how hairy I am, and how my nose is broad like my father's, and what a shame it was I didn't get "the Macintyre cheekbones." I was also tired of watching Grandma pick on Mom, asking if Mom was dating anybody and suggesting ways she could make herself more attractive.

"Why do you even want to go?" I asked Mom.

She laughed. "I ask myself that all the time." But when she saw that I was serious, she continued. "Well," she said, "I've been going to Fire Island in the summer since I was a kid. I love the ocean, and the deer, and the swans, and the peacefulness . . ."

The peacefulness, which lasted until Grandma's second drink was getting low.

"I like the community," Mom went on. "I like getting out of the city when it's boiling hot. And I thought you loved going out there, being by the ocean. I know Penguin does. Don't you, Poo-Poo?" She reached down and patted him on his chubby back. Penguin wiggled in pleasure, probably thinking of chasing seagulls on the beach.

Mom was right. I did love playing in the ocean and looking for perfect shells and making "sandcastles" that always came out the same: a formless pile of sand with a trench in front and a seagull feather on top. "Aunt Jenny loved it, too," I said.

"She sure did. Remember how she'd go into the ocean, even if the water was freezing?"

"And then she'd drip the freezing water all over everybody."

Aunt Jenny didn't spend the whole summer with us at Grandma's. She just joined us for a week or two, if she could. Mom loved it when Aunt Jenny was there, because Aunt Jenny knew how to flatter or distract Grandma whenever she started to get mean. Aunt Jenny would say something like "Diane, you were so right about that new house on Lewis Walk. It's simply atrocious. Who did you say the owners were? They must be ghastly."

And Grandma would forget about Mom for a minute and start ragging on the neighbors. "The Greniers! Ucch, they're terrible. They leave their garbage cans uncovered, and the deer get into the trash . . ."

Mom changed the subject away from Aunt

Jenny. "Is there something else you want to do instead of going to the beach? I know you're a little too old to get excited about summer camp. But maybe there's a theater camp or a writing program we could find for you in the city. I bet they'd love to have you volunteer more hours at Waggytail, too."

"Mmmm." Now that she mentioned it, the idea of hanging around the hot, stinky city with nothing to do didn't sound so appealing.

"We don't have to spend the whole summer on Fire Island," she continued. "Look, we're going out there soon to help Grandma open the house for the season—let's see how we feel about it and then make summer plans. Do you want me to ask Savvy's moms if she can come?"

I shrugged. The fewer words I said about Savvy, the better.

Mom decided to dig a little. "How is Savvy?"

"She's . . . okay."

Mom bent down to untangle Penguin's leash,

which was wound around one of his back legs. "Seems like you two aren't hanging out as much."

"Yeah, she's been . . . busy with stuff."

"Stuff?"

I used my mom's phone and showed her a picture from Savvy's Instagram. She was posing with Naturi and Sierra in front of a subway poster that said JUICY.

"I see," said Mom. "Very busy indeed."

"It's like a full-time job," I explained. "Being juicy."

"Oh, juiciness doesn't just happen," Mom agreed. "You have to put the work into it."

"Her project for current events is called 'Juiciness, and How It Affects Today's Teens.' "

"When she gets to college, she can major in being juicy."

"With a minor in juiciness studies."

This was the kind of thing we used to do with Aunt Jenny all the time, take an idea and see how silly we could get with it, the three of us challenging each other to new levels of ridiculousness.

Aunt Jenny Aunt Jenny Aunt Jenny Aunt Jenny Aunt Jenny Aunt Jenny Aunt Jenny Aunt Jenny Aunt Jenny Aunt Jenny Aunt Jenny Aunt Jenny Aunt Jenny Aunt Jenny Aunt Jenny.

No wonder people said I'm depressing and boring.

Four

DAY 3 OF MY LUCKY MONTH STARTED poorly. There was the usual dog-snot issue, and then I dropped my phone in the toilet. (At least the toilet was flushed.) My phone was only in there for a second before I grabbed it, so it would probably survive, but I would have to wipe it down with alcohol and let it sit in a bag of dry rice all day.

"See?" said Mom when I got back from walking Penguin. "Aren't you glad that wasn't a six-hundred-dollar phone?"

Great. Now she had an excuse to never get me a new phone. I would be stuck forever with my crappy one. I should have flushed it when I had the chance. "Shut up," I muttered.

She narrowed her eyes at me. "I know you didn't just tell me to shut up. I know you value your life too much for that."

I wasn't in the mood for my mom that morning. I grabbed Penguin's collar to detach the leash and he yelped in surprise. "Whatever."

"HEY," she said, extra loud. "Don't you EVER jerk him around by the collar. And don't you EVER tell me to shut up. I don't tell you to shut up. That's not how we speak to each other."

"Okay, then, BE QUIET." That was something she said plenty of times.

From the look on her face, and the lovely red color rising there, I knew I had made a big mistake. I dropped my head, ready for her to scream at me, but to my surprise she closed her eyes and took a deep breath. She was probably thinking of ways to punish me–usually she took away my phone for a day, but my phone was already busted, so that wouldn't work. I sneaked a peek at her face to see how badly I'd upset her.

Her jaw was trembling and her eyes were filling with tears. She grabbed a paper towel from the counter and crushed it against her face. I could see her shoulders shaking like she was crying, but she was silent.

If she wanted to make me feel guilty, it wasn't going to work. I stomped out of the room and collected my stuff for school.

When I passed through the kitchen to leave, she was still standing in the same place against the counter.

"Look at me," she demanded. I did. Her eyes were red and wet, but her stare was steady. She was *pissed.*

"Ever since Aunt Jenny died, I've been trying to go easy on you, because I know you're hurting. But I am *not* going to let you get away with acting like a brat. You are pushing your luck. You feel me? And your luck is running out."

I hate it when Mom tries to be cool and say things like "You feel me?"

"Okay," I said. "I'm sorry. Now can I go?"

I was halfway down the stairs by the time her words reached my brain: *And your luck is running out.*

No kidding. My aunt was dead, my best friend was ditching me for the popular girls, and now I had no phone for the day. Aside from a cursed $20, a seat on the bus, and Doggie Lancelot's recovery, what had all my supposed luck brought me?

I resolved to forget about the letter. It was a stupid mind game, just like everything else.

✉

Savvy wasn't outside of school when I got there. That was probably a good thing. I was still pissed off by the texts I'd gotten the day before—even if she didn't send them, like she said, her friends did. She was hanging out with people who were nasty to me for no reason, and I was sick of it.

I didn't know who to stand with on the sidewalk. I didn't even have my phone, so I felt even more awkward. I tried not to watch Dakota's squad in their thick cluster: Sierra, Naturi, Tyler, Lewis, and the two or three others who got the privilege of hanging out with them this semester. They were definitely watching me, though, and Sierra purposely said the word "pathetic" loud enough for me to hear it.

Savvy hadn't shown up by the time we had to go inside. As we were walking in, Dakota and Sierra passed right by me, holding a loud conversation meant for my ears.

"That's so awesome that Savvy hooked up with Tyler yesterday," said Sierra.

"I know," Dakota said. "She's perfect for him."

They turned my way and smirked, then walked on.

Savvy hooked up with Tyler yesterday. I could

barely breathe. I felt like I couldn't walk. Luckily, I was right next to the first-floor teachers' bathroom, and the door was slightly open. I slipped inside and locked it behind me.

I let out all my breath at once. I was safe in there—nobody was going to walk in, nobody could hear me. I sat down on the lid of the toilet. I was so frustrated, I wanted to bang my head against the wall. Instead, I exploded into angry tears.

WHY, I thought, weeping bitterly. *WHY IS THIS HAPPENING TO ME.* Hadn't I had enough already? I just lost someone I'd loved all my life, someone I could always count on, my second mom. And this was after months of watching her trying to fight, getting sicker and thinner and weaker until she wasn't there anymore.

ENOUGH. I get it, Universe. You can stop now. I didn't need to be losing Savvy so soon after losing Aunt Jenny. And she didn't need to hook up with the guy I'd liked for *two entire years,* even if Tyler started it. You never hook up with your best friend's crush! That's the very first rule of girl code! And the whole Dakota group didn't need to laugh at me. And Mom didn't need to be on my case. And I *really* didn't need some mind-game mystery letter telling me I was lucky when clearly I was not.

I felt very sorry for myself. I knew I wasn't supposed to, because I had a lot of privileges other kids didn't, but sometimes it happened anyway. I wasn't living in a refugee camp or a hut with a hole for a toilet, but my life still sucked. I cried and cried until I was empty, which took a while. I had to make sure that no more tears could come out of me in front of other people. Only then could I leave the bathroom.

I showed up five minutes late to history, fake-sneezing to cover for my puffy eyes. "Allergies," I said apologetically. *"Achoo!"*

I kept up the allergies charade throughout the day, and every chance I got, I went to the bathroom and pressed cold, wet paper towels on my eyes. I decided to spend lunch in the library so I wouldn't have to see Savvy. She'd probably be sitting with Tyler as cartoon hearts exploded over their heads. I knew it wasn't her fault that Tyler liked her and not me, but it still fully sucked for me. Was I just supposed to sit there, one table away, while Savvy sat between Dakota and Tyler, her new best friend and her new boyfriend?

She could at least have told me about her and Tyler herself.

It was hard not being able to text her. I kept imagining myself typing things and erasing them without sending. I thought maybe if we could talk about it, if she could explain what happened or apologize, some of the furious nausea inside me might go away. But the texts I got from her the day before were fresh in my mind:

u don't know when ur not wanted

go away

I could not cry in the library. I would not cry in the library. I was not crying in the library. It was very dusty in there. Did I mention my allergies?

After lunch I was waiting for science lab to start when there was an announcement over the loudspeaker, saying that the auditions for the play were rescheduled for that afternoon instead of Friday.

Great. So now I would get to show off my puffy red eyes to the whole world.

✉

When I got to the auditorium after last period, I looked better than I had in the morning, but I still appeared highly allergic to life.

I waited for my turn in the back row, looking over the scene Ms. Engel gave us to read. It was a scene where a daughter was arguing with her father. I ran through the lines a few times out loud so I wouldn't stumble on any words. This girl Brooke, the only person in our class who could read aloud from *Romeo and Juliet* and make it sound halfway understandable, was urgently whispering the lines to herself with her eyes closed. She was pretty much guaranteed to get the lead role.

When it was my turn to take the stage, right before I opened my mouth, somebody made the sad-trombone sound that means "loser." Then there was a bunch of giggling. If Ms. Engel heard it, she didn't say anything.

I felt hot and sweaty, like I'd just run a race, and my heart was pounding. When I started reading the lines from the script, they came out louder than I meant them to.

"'You don't understand,'" I began. "'You tell me I'm your whole life. You tell me every morning and every night, "Nadine, you're my whole life." But you're not *my* whole life. I want to have a life of my own!'"

I realized I was shouting, and the script didn't say anything about shouting. But Ms. Engel looked pleased, and it sounded kind of cool, echoing in the auditorium, so I went with it.

"'You have to let me breathe! Ever since Mom died, you've been . . .'"

Gulp. The words stuck in my throat. What was happening? I heard Mom's words from that morning: *Ever since Aunt Jenny died . . .*

I started the line over. "'Ever since Mom died . . .'"

I said a quick prayer. *Please don't make me break down in the middle of my audition and start bawling like a baby.* But the tears started to come.

I swallowed hard and kept going. "'. . . you've been so angry at me. You act like I'm a bad daughter, but I'm not.'"

Ms. Engel read the father's line: "'I never said that, Nadine. You're my—'"

"'WHOLE LIFE,'" I read, cutting her off. "'I know! And *my* whole life is about to begin. You have to let me start it.'"

"'I can't let you get hurt. I can't lose you.'" Ms. Engel finished the father's line and just looked at me.

From the back of the auditorium I heard someone clapping very slowly. It sounded sarcastic. I wanted to throw up. I knew I deserved to be mocked for my disastrous yelling, crying audition, but I wasn't sure how much more mocking I could take.

Then the clap began moving toward the stage, into the lights, and after I wiped my tears I could see the person behind it. It was none other than Melanie Lambright, the junior who had written *Umbilical.*

Melanie was big and tall and dressed dramatically in all black, with pink streaks in her hair. I didn't know her–eighth graders and eleventh graders don't mix–but everybody knew who she was from last year's school talent show, when she performed a monologue she wrote about a crazy rich woman on the subway. It was weird and funny and contained a few choice bits of adult language, which made her a hero in our eyes.

As Melanie walked down the aisle, still slowly clapping, she kept her eyes fixed on me. Finally, she stopped in front of the stage and frowned.

"Who are you," she demanded. It was a statement, not a question.

"I'm . . . Emma," I said nervously. "Macintyre."

I wanted to get off the stage, out of the lights. Other people were waiting for their turn. I knew the mocking noises would start up again any second. Melanie just stared at me. I wasn't sure if it was a good stare or a bad stare.

"That was incredible," she said.

Ms. Engel nodded in agreement. "Remarkable. Great job."

I thought I might collapse with relief. "Th-thank you," I stuttered.

Melanie and Ms. Engel whispered to each other for a second. Ms. Engel smiled, and suddenly all the whispering about me that had happened earlier that day didn't matter. I was "incredible," "remarkable," and "great." I walked off the stage with my head high.

Brooke grabbed my arm as I passed her seat. "Emma," she said sternly, "you were so good. I hate you and everything about you."

From Brooke, this was a compliment.

"Thanks," I said, grinning, as I left the auditorium. "I hope you break your leg."

✉

I walked home from school slowly. As I got closer to our building, the great feeling from the audition began to wear off. I definitely wasn't eager to see Mom after that morning's argument. I hoped she'd be at a meeting, but there she was, sitting in front of her laptop in the kitchen.

"Bloop." Her voice sounded mellow, which meant she'd probably just gotten home from AA. "How was your day?"

"Sucked," I said. Then I reconsidered. "Except auditions."

"Yeah?" She closed the laptop and smiled. "You did well?"

"I think so. I don't know. Ms. Engel said I was great."

"Bloop! I'm so glad to hear it."

I loved it when Mom and I make up from a fight without talking about it. Then we can just act like it didn't happen and move on. Now, *this* was the kind of luck I liked. The day had started out rocky, then got rockier, but then it started to smooth out. Maybe it could be salvaged after all.

I looked around for the container of rice with my phone in it. "Where's my phone?" I asked.

"It's right here," Mom said, and reached into the cupboard. She handed me a smooth white box, still in the cellophane.

A brand-new phone.

My jaw hit the floor so hard I nearly broke my own foot. "Are you kidding me?"

I was astonished. The *last* thing I expected after the fight that morning was to come home and find a new phone. Was Mom trying to make a point? Was she about to take it back and tell me I was too immature for it, and say I had to wait until August to get a new phone, like she'd been saying?

I gaped at her.

She smiled. "It's yours. Open it."

I started unwrapping it, unfurling its charger, feeling its weight in my hand. I wished I could get video of myself unboxing it. It was SO much nicer than my old phone. I couldn't wait to get it set up and start playing with it.

But first I gave Mom a hug. "Mom! You are blowing minds here! You are the most legit mom ever!"

"You're welcome, and I know."

I let go of her and went back to caressing my lovely new phone. My old case wouldn't fit, but I'd get a new one—a few new ones, to switch up according to my mood.

Mom said, "I'll help you write a thank-you note to Herbie. He gave it to me."

Herbie was one of her clients. Mom met him when she was volunteering at the library with a group that does tech support for elderly people, teaching them how to use email and helping them with the gadgets their well-meaning grandkids forced on them. Then Herbie became a paying client, hiring Mom to come to his apartment once every other week, for "maintenance," which mostly meant listening to him complain about technology and talk about the good old days.

I met Herbie once when Mom took me to the volunteer group's annual party. He and I sat at a table together while everyone else was dancing and mingling, and he told me some jokes I didn't fully understand but knew I probably shouldn't be hearing. Then he gave me ten bucks and told me to go buy myself a nice cigar. Herbie was super old, like almost ninety, but he was awesome. Mom said he always tried to overpay her and act like it was a mistake.

Mom continued. “He says his grandnephew gave it to him.” She switched into an imitation of Herbie’s voice. “What the hell do I need this for? He wants me to start online dating?”

I clutched the phone to my chest. “He’s not going to want it back, is he?”

She laughed and shook her head no. “Herbie practically threw it at me when I saw him today. ‘Get it away from me! You know what these things do? They suck your soul out through your eyeballs.’ His grandnephew wanted him to have it so they could FaceTime. Herbie says, ‘I already learned the Skype. I’m not learning anything else that’s new.’ ”

“You swear this is mine?” I asked. “I won’t have to give it back?” I didn’t mention that I couldn’t possibly give it back because it had already fused to my hand. The phone and I had become one. “What’s the catch?”

“No catch. Except if you lose it, you don’t get a nice new one to replace it. You can go back to your old phone.”

She handed me the container of rice with my old phone in it. My old phone—it had seen me through so much. I felt a little guilty, knowing that I was about to cast it aside.

Oh well!

I played with the new phone all night, downloading apps and testing them out. I was so engrossed, I didn't realize until I was drifting off to sleep:

I'd just gotten item number 1 on my luck list.

Five

MY GOOD-LUCK STREAK CONTINUED THE next morning. I'd been dreading the sight of Savvy and Tyler on the sidewalk outside school, but there was no sign of Savvy, at least not from a distance. As soon as I got close, Brooke the Drama Star and her friend Harrison pulled me over to stand with them.

"You have to help us," said Brooke. "Mr. Auchen's mole needs a name."

"Um, why?" I asked. Like there would be a logical reason to name a mole.

"Because it's practically an independent being," explained Harrison. "Therefore, it deserves a name."

Harrison had been Brooke's best friend since fifth grade. They were by far the smartest kids in our class, and they were always together—before school, at lunch, during any free period. He was the only person allowed to call Brooke by her given name, Brooklyn, and he was weirdly possessive of that privilege. I couldn't tell if he was gay, in love with her, or both.

"How about Dobby the Face Mole?" suggested Brooke.

Harrison put his hand on his chin in an exaggerated I'm-thinking pose. "I don't know," he said. "I'm leaning toward Bernice."

"Call it Guaca," I said. "Then its full name will be Guaca Mole."

Brooke opened her eyes wide. "Emma Macintyre! You are today's winner of Name That Mole!"

✉

Not only was Savvy missing from the sidewalk that morning, but she wasn't in homeroom and didn't appear in class. Tyler Hoff didn't seem to care. I saw him before social studies, massaging the shoulders of notorious airhead Venice Biandi, who Lewis had once described as "a walking blond joke." I had a brief flash of hope that maybe the thing Tyler had with Savvy wasn't a thing after all.

Right before lunch, the cast list for the play was posted outside Ms. Engel's classroom. Everybody was crowded around it, so I couldn't see anything. I heard Brooke say "Yes!" so I figured she got either the lead or the part of the dead mom, which was almost as good. She ran off with Harrison to celebrate. Then this girl Azalia turned and gave me a death glare as she walked away. "*Good luck*, Emma."

I shimmied into the open spot, scanned the list, and gasped. So that's why Azalia tried to jinx me.

I got the lead. Me. The lead part. I got it.

Brooke was playing the mom.

Like with my new phone, I didn't want to believe it was real without proof. People around me were saying congratulations, some of them sarcastic, some of them sincere. I heard someone repeat the news to the people behind them: "Emma's the girl, Carter's the dad, and Brooke's the dead mom." But I still couldn't believe I'd actually gotten the lead part. I thought for sure I'd wind up playing one of the neighbors or, like, Townsperson #2, which is the role I usually get.

I checked the list again, drawing a line with my finger from NADINE to EMMA MACINTYRE, making sure I'd read it correctly and I hadn't been cast to play the father.

"Okay, good for you, let someone else see now." Lewis the Troll pushed past me to look for his name. "Yes!"

He had been cast to play Julian. I didn't know what that meant, but his name was not far below mine and Carter's, so I guessed it was a decent-sized part.

Venice Biandi, the ditz with the massage-able shoulders, came up to me and started gushing. "I knew you were going to get it," she said, launching into her usual mile-a-minute monologue. "You were amazing at the audition. You should see if they recorded it." She stuck to me, continuing to jabber as the crowd moved toward the lunch room. "If you put it on YouTube, you never know who could see it. My sister's friend got to be in a commercial because of her YouTube. Now she's gonna maybe move to L.A., and we're gonna visit to, like, scope it out . . ."

Venice sat down at the far end of the Dakota table, where she'd started eating lunch lately, hoping to make her way toward a top seat. Since she and I were talking with each other, I sat down next to her. I felt weird about sitting at their table, since they had made it so clear that I was unwanted, but they just ignored the fact that I was there. I kept waiting for Savvy to show up, but she must have been absent again.

Down at the other end of the table, Lewis was crowing about his success.

"I'm gonna *kill* this part. Watch. I'm gonna *murder* it. I'm going to *exterminate* it."

Dakota, Naturi, and Sierra were humoring him, but they seemed to be distracted by something on their phones. A few bits of conversation drifted my way.

"She didn't."

"She did."

"Stop."

"I can't imagine it."

"You're kidding me."

For once, it didn't seem like they were talking about me. By some good fortune, there was another girl they'd decided to torture that day. Whoever it was, I didn't envy her.

✉

That afternoon in English, while Madelyn Michaud was giving an endless, grinding presentation on the epic greatness of her personal heroes, the 2016 U.S. Olympic women's gymnastics team, I started thinking about my luck list. I was only a few days into my lucky month, but I already knew I needed to make a few changes.

For starts, I had to cross out number 3:

> ~~3. Dakota likes me and invites me to hang out at her house with everyone.~~

I no longer wanted Dakota to like me, which was handy, because that was never going to happen. She acted as if she didn't even like her own friends most of the time—they were always being "such dumpster fires" or "total garbage people." I still envied Dakota, the way most of the girls in our class did, for her thick hair and her unholy self-confidence and her absentee parents, but I no longer wanted to hang out at her house. My new number 3 was literally the opposite of that:

> **3.** Dakota leaves me alone.

While I was thinking about my list, I decided to cross out number 4, too:

~~4. Make out with Tyler Hoff.~~

And change it to:

4. Make out with a guy I like.

Rest in peace, my crush on Tyler Hoff, for you are dead to me now.

It was a solemn and historic moment, me giving up this two-year romantic fantasy–truly, this was the end of an era. If this had happened two months ago, I could be commemorating it with Savvy and a ceremonial tub of ice cream.

Speaking of Savvy, there was number 9 on my list:

9. Savvy stops being weird to me.

I wasn't ready to cross this one out.

I mean, obviously, she didn't want to be best friends anymore. Obviously, she had a whole new set of friends, including the guy I used to be in love with, the one she "hooked up" with, whatever that meant. But just hours before that happened, Savvy and I ate lunch together like always. What was I supposed to think? She wasn't acting like herself lately, but she was still Savvy—the same Savvy who I'd been having sleepovers with since we were eight years old. Savvy, whose bedroom in our thirty-room mansion had a secret passageway behind the fireplace that connected to the fireplace in mine. Savvy, who had been there squeezing my hand at Aunt Jenny's funeral. She and her moms were part of my family.

I'd given up hope of joining Savvy in the Dakota group. But I didn't want to give up on our friendship. Mom and Aunt Jenny used to tell the story about the time when they were in their twenties and had a fight over a guy, and they didn't talk to each other for *three years.* Then Aunt Jenny's dad died, and she called Mom, and they made up right away and became best friends again. They always laughed when they told the story of the fight, because that's how silly they were to let a guy come between them.

Things could still work out with Savvy. Maybe our friendship wouldn't go back to being the way it was before, but I had faith in the lucky letter. In less than one week, I'd gotten a new phone and the lead in the play, and those were two major *things I wanted to happen.* And I'd been even luckier than I'd hoped. I'd only asked for a speaking part in the play, and I'd gotten the biggest speaking part in the whole show.

I thought back to the day of the audition, and how unlucky I'd felt going into it. I'd thought it was the worst possible luck that the auditions had been moved to the exact day when I was a total mess. I didn't feel lucky when I almost embarrassed myself in front of everybody by bawling onstage. But what if I'd been in a better mood that day? Would I still have gotten the part if I hadn't been so upset?

The letter said that some things would be *obvious right away*, while other things would *take time to reveal themselves.*

Like getting the lead in the show.

Funny, I thought, *how unlucky events can lead to lucky ones.*

✉

Now that I had some proof that the letter was really lucky, I didn't want to waste any time or overlook any chances. Time to take Ms. Engel's advice and buy some raffle tickets.

Mom was working at the kitchen table when I came home that afternoon wearing my best I-want-something smile. She didn't even have to look up at me to know that I was scheming. "What do you want?" she asked.

"Mom, awesome Mom, most legit Mom, will you please buy me some scratch-off lottery tickets?"

Two years ago, Aunt Jenny let me use the edge of a dime to scratch the silver coating off her lottery ticket, and I fell in love with the idea of winning free money. I wanted my own scratch-offs, but I couldn't buy them for myself, because it's gambling, and I was under 18. So I had to rely on sympathetic adults. I showed Mom the cash and prayed that she was feeling sympathetic.

She was not. "No more scratch-offs! Grandma gave you all that money for your twelfth birthday, and you spent the whole thing on the lottery. I don't even know how you managed that."

I'd given my birthday money from Grandma to Aunt Jenny so she could buy some scratch-offs for me. I got $20 worth of tickets, thinking that at least one of them had to be lucky. I'd sat down at our table and scratched and scratched, but all I got was a pile of silver coating.

"That was almost a year ago! Please? Even just one? It's important."

She raised an eyebrow at me. "What's so important? You owe money to your bookie? You need to bail somebody out of prison?"

I tried not to roll my eyes in frustration. "Okay, it's not *important.* I just . . . I have a lucky feeling."

Mom debated it silently for a minute, then said, "All right. You promise to walk Penguin the next three nights after dinner, and I'll get you one ticket."

Penguin always gets excited at his name. I was just as excited. "Yes yes yes," I agreed, handing her the money, and Penguin and I rolled around on the floor for the ninety-nine hours it took for Mom to get her shoes on, go to the bodega on the corner, and return with a scratch ticket.

"Here you go," she said, handing it to me. "Don't ask me for another for at least six months."

"Thank you thank you thank you thank you thank you," I said, already scratching at the silver.

The game was to scratch off the squares and hope to find matching numbers. If I uncovered a match, I could win as little as one dollar and as much as ten thousand. I started scratching, and right away I had a match.

This was *really good* luck.

Mom laughed in surprise. "You won!"

But how much did I win? The amount was hidden under the silver coating. I couldn't scratch fast enough. I knew it would tell me that I'd won the ten thousand dollars.

I won ten bucks.

I was confused, and a little let down. I thought my good luck meant I'd win the big jackpot. I mean, ten bucks is great and all, but not when you expect ten thousand.

Mom saw the look on my face and stared at me strangely. "You just won! You should be dancing with joy!"

Oh, right. I had to act normal so I wouldn't give away the secret to Mom the Human Person. "Yeah! Woo!" I smiled wide and pumped my fist. "Lucky me."

She relaxed. Now I was acting like the kid she knew. "I'll cash it in for you tomorrow. But that's it! I know it feels great to win, but you're not going to win every time. And the last thing I need is a twelve-year-old with a gambling problem."

I nodded and hugged her. "Thanks, Moop." Then I went back to my room.

✉

As Week 1 wore into Week 2, I kept noticing how good luck led to more good luck: getting the part in the play led to new friends, which led to focusing less on old friends. We cast members bonded pretty hard—hanging out in the morning, sitting together at lunch, group-texting each other all the time. Rehearsals were so much fun, we didn't want to leave the auditorium when we were done, which was how some of us got in the habit of stopping by Brooke's afterward to keep our (usually ridiculous) conversation going a while longer.

I had so many new friends, Mom had to keep making me start stories over: "Wait, which one is Brooke again? And who's Geneva?"

I showed her a picture on my phone, taken the day before. "Brooke's the one holding the snake. She's best friends with Harrison—he's been in love with her forever. The whole reason he's stage-managing the show is so he can be around her during rehearsals without having to be in the play. Geneva's the one with the braids and she's in love with Harrison, so this morning she was telling me how she was having a bunch of people over on Friday . . . Oh, can I hang out at Geneva's on Friday after school? We don't have rehearsal. So she's thinking about telling him then, but I said she should talk to Brooke first, because Brooke would know if Harrison likes her or not . . ."

Yeah, I didn't blame Mom for being confused. It was a complicated set of relationships. I was still puzzling them out myself.

Lewis hung out with the rest of the cast a little bit, but he still sat with Tyler and Dakota at lunch. They didn't appreciate his new after-school interests. The one and only time Lewis started walking toward the cast table at lunch, Tyler yelled out, "Where you going, Lew-zer?" And Lewis instantly turned and went to his usual seat.

I was starting to suspect that Lewis was almost not awful, as long as he was away from his awful friends.

🖂

On Lucky Day 9, Lewis and I were backstage together at rehearsal while Ms. Engel and Melanie discussed the blocking for the next scene, and I saw him fiddling with some loose script pages, folding and tearing them randomly. But when he finished folding, I saw it wasn't random at all. He'd made an origami frog.

I forgot that Lewis used to do origami. Back in the third grade, he would fold any piece of paper he could grab, even if it was your language arts worksheet. I remember untwisting a spelling quiz of mine after he'd made it into a rose and presented it to me with pride. "I can't believe you undid it," he sulked, even though I had to so I could see which words I misspelled. He never made an origami rose for me again.

Lewis saw me notice the frog in his hand, and he looked mortified. He clenched his fist and squished the frog into a ball, then threw it on the floor.

I cringed. "Why did you—" I started to ask, but he turned and walked away.

Okay, here's a thing about me: I have a really hard time with inanimate objects that are shaped like animals and/or have faces. I am aware that, in reality, a teddy bear is not alive and doesn't have feelings, because it's basically a pillow with googly eyes glued on it. I don't feel guilty about throwing my pillow on the floor, so why do I have to pick up the teddy bear if it falls on the floor and place it carefully back on its spot on my bed and apologize to it in my mind? (Not that I have a teddy bear on my bed or anything.) People can throw all the science in the world at me, and I will agree with them all day long: Stuffed animals are not alive. These are facts. But I'm still going to apologize to the bear.

So I felt bad for the poor squished frog on the floor. I picked it up and tried to uncrumple it. I noticed that it was made out of a script page from Act III, where Julian helps Nadine leave their small town because he wants her to pursue her dreams, even though it means she is leaving him. He's saying goodbye to her at the bus station.

NADINE

Come with me.

JULIAN

I can't.

NADINE

You keep telling me I can leave—why can't you?

JULIAN

I'm not as brave as you.

I'm not as brave as you. This line was circled a few times in messy black ink.

We were encouraged by Ms. Engel to take notes on our scripts. We wrote down notes on the blocking (*upstage left*), the directions we received (*go louder here, then pause*), and any ideas we might have that would bring us "closer to the truth of the character" (*Nadine = angry at mom for dying*).

I'm not as brave as you. I wondered what made Lewis circle that one line. Lewis wasn't a coward. He talked a lot of trash about people, but he did it right to their faces, even if they were bigger than him. And he never backed down, no matter what punishment he faced. He was obnoxious and stubborn and infuriating at times, but he was brave about it.

I refolded the frog along its creases as best I could and put it carefully in my backpack. I reassured it in my mind: *You're safe now, little frog.*

✉

I was coming home after rehearsal the next day when I saw Fran the Super in front of the building, about to light a cigarette. Fran smokes all the time, so her breath smells like a dirty ashtray and her fingers are brown and yellow from the tar. It's fairly disgusting. Other than that, she's cool.

"Hey, kid."

"Hey."

Then I had a thought. Maybe Fran knew something about the letter. Even if she wasn't the person who left it, she might have seen or heard something that could lead to the person who did.

"Um," I said, thinking quickly. "Mom said to tell you, the towel rack in the bathroom is loose."

"Well, I was gonna kill myself slowly with this thing." She tucked the unlit cigarette back into the pack and shoved it in her pocket. "But let's get a look at that towel rack."

She tromped up the stairs in her work boots, little clouds of dust coming off her with every step. I followed behind, trying not to inhale too deeply.

The towel rack truly was loose, not that Mom or I cared. Fran looked at it, then back at me. "That's it? You just gotta tighten these two nuts here. Where's your wrench?"

This was going to be a quick job. I had to find a way to bring up the letter. I shrugged, stalling for time.

Fran went into the kitchen and opened a few drawers, looking for the tool she needed. "Find the wrench," she muttered to herself. "Then I can smoke this Lucky."

THAT WORD!

"What did you say?" I asked.

Fran found the wrench. She flipped it in the air and caught it smoothly by its handle. "Said this'll take two seconds, then I'm gonna smoke."

"I thought you said something about luck."

Fran applied her magic to the towel rack. Somehow, though she was not working on the plumbing, her plumber's butt managed to peek out the back of her pants. Maybe it happened automatically every time she entered a bathroom.

"That's my brand," she explained. She pulled the pack from her pocket to show me. "Lucky Strikes."

"Oh," I said, disappointed. It was just a coincidence.

"Your mom's friend used to nag me. 'There's

no such thing as a lucky cigarette. Every cigarette is bad luck.' "

Mom's friend. I felt a *zing!* run through my whole body. Out of nowhere, Fran had brought up the subject of Aunt Jenny. Maybe it wasn't coincidence after all.

"Aunt Jenny," I said. "She talked a lot about luck. Like, in horoscopes, how certain days were 'more favorable' than others . . ."

"Yeah, yeah." Fran was finished, but she leaned back against the wall with a smile on her face, obviously thinking of Aunt Jenny. "I don't believe that garbage about horoscopes or fortune-telling or hanging a horseshoe right-side up for luck."

"You don't?"

"Nah. The way I see it, you're either lucky or you're not. It's got nothing to do with the planets. It doesn't go up and down, like the stock market. You're born with it. You born starving in Siberia? You got bad luck. You born with bad health? Also bad luck. The rest of us? We got it good. If you're not struggling to survive, you got it good. End of story."

I had no idea Fran was such a philosopher. I was trying to make sense of what she was saying when she spoke again.

"Jenny . . ." Fran cleared her throat a little.

I couldn't tell if she was sad from saying Aunt Jenny's name or if she just had gunk in her throat.

"Jenny had good luck. She had a happy life. A lot of friends. It ended too soon."

We were quiet. Fran cleared her throat again. She took out a cigarette and looked at it like she wished Aunt Jenny were there to nag her about it.

Then she sighed. "Might as well join her."

✉

When Mom got back from her meeting a half hour later, she was delighted with the new, stable towel rack. "I didn't even realize how much it was annoying me until you got it fixed."

I had learned a few things from my time with Fran: (1) A wrench is used for tightening bolts. (2) Fran did not believe in any "garbage" about horoscopes, fortunes, or luck. Which meant that (3) Fran had not written the letter.

Six

THE FOLLOWING DAY, SOMEONE FROM Mom's volunteer group at the library called to tell her that Herbie died. Bad luck, especially for Herbie.

Mom was sad but not surprised. "Well," she said, sighing as she told me the news, "he *was* eighty-six. And from all the stories he told me, it sounded like he had a great life. And he went quickly, in his sleep, after watching the Yankees win, so I know he was happy."

Mom and I were invited to the memorial service. I didn't want to go. I went to Aunt Jenny's memorial service, and that was enough memorial services for the rest of my life. I spent the whole time furious—after their tearful speeches, Derek and Brik and a lot of Aunt Jenny's best friends were laughing and telling jokes and talking to each other about things that had nothing to do with Aunt Jenny. It wasn't supposed to be a party.

✉

So Mom attended Herbie's memorial alone. Afterward, she came home with a strange look on her face.

"Herbie left me some stuff," she said, puzzled.

My ears perked up, just like Penguin's do. "What kind of stuff? Where is it?"

"A couple of boxes. They're at his apartment uptown. His grandnephew Darren from North Carolina is staying there, packing up and sorting everything out. He says we can go to the apartment this weekend and pick up . . . whatever it is."

A couple of boxes? Was that a *bunch* of boxes or a *few* boxes? "How many? And what's in the boxes?"

She shook her head. "I don't know. Darren just said some boxes. He doesn't even know what's in them. He said they're heavy, though, so it's probably books."

"Or gold bullion," I said optimistically. Who knew? Maybe one of the boxes was full of money. Then Herbie's death would be good luck. Not for Herbie, of course. I didn't love the idea of someone's death bringing good luck to me. Then again, I didn't kill Herbie.

✉

The next day, we rode the train up to Herbie's apartment in Harlem. We spent the trip talking about the boxes.

"What would be the least convenient kind of box?" asked Mom. "Because I'm sure that's what they'll turn out to be."

"A box made of marble?" I suggested.

"A box made of lead?"

"A box made of some outer-space material where one particle of it weighs a thousand pounds?"

"A box made out of a million boxes?"

We went on like this all the way to 125th Street, suggesting boxes made out of cooked spaghetti, butterfly wings, fine crystal, air. We mimed handing each other air boxes.

"Boxes made out of used diapers," I said.

"He better not have left me any boxes of adult diapers," Mom said.

Herbie's "apartment" turned out to be a whole brownstone building, four floors and a small backyard. There was a moving/storage truck parked outside. A short guy was trying to carry a table down the stairs, but the table was too big and heavy for him alone. Mom ran up and grabbed the other end of the table, and they carried it down cautiously, step by step.

"Thanks," the guy said, mopping his face with his T-shirt. "My great-uncle only bought furniture made of lead."

I shot a look at Mom—we were just joking about the boxes being lead!—but she wasn't looking at me. She was looking at the mad abdominals the guy exposed while wiping his face.

"Hey, Darren, this is my daughter, Emma. Emma, this is Darren, Herbie's grandnephew. We met at the memorial service yesterday, and he told me about the boxes Herbie left for you and me."

Darren turned to me. "So you're the one who wound up with the phone."

I hoped he wasn't mad at me because Herbie gave away his expensive gift.

But he smiled and said, "I'm glad it went to someone who could operate it."

It was obvious that Darren was overwhelmed with getting everything down to the truck, so we got out of the way. Mom and I went into the near-empty building and started looking at all the boxes. There were at least twenty of them, and they were all unmarked. Since we couldn't tell which ones were ours, we sat down on a window seat and waited for Darren to be done.

But that was going to take a while. In between lugging furniture and dealing with the guys in the truck, his phone kept ringing. As soon as the truck pulled away, we heard him call someone back.

"Pauline," he said. He was outside on the stoop, but the windows were open, and we could hear him clearly. "Stop it. I told you, I'm not having this talk until I get home. Pauline . . . Pauline!"

Mom smirked at me and I smirked back. People with girlfriends or boyfriends were always arguing on the phone.

"Yes," he shouted. "I *did* tell you how long I was going to be away, when I told you I DIDN'T KNOW HOW LONG I WAS GOING TO BE AWAY!"

Mom and I were both highly amused. I stifled a laugh, which turned into a snort.

"I'm hanging up now. And I'm turning off my phone for the rest of the day."

Darren came back inside the house, and we tried to pretend we hadn't been listening. Our faces must have told him otherwise.

"Uh, that was a business thing," he said, embarrassed. "Let me get you some water. All I have are plastic cups—everything else is packed."

Darren got us cups of water from the kitchen and rejoined us in the bare living room. We took our cups and thanked him.

"I didn't get a chance to tell you at the memorial," he said to Mom, "but Uncle Herb talked about you a lot. He called you Katie, Katie, the Computer Lady."

Mom laughed. "I don't know why I let him call me that. I never let anybody call me Katie."

"Yeah, Uncle Herb got away with murder. You know, he loved being in his eighties, because anytime somebody asked him to do something, all he had to say was . . ."

Mom chimed in and they said it together: " 'Leave me alone, I'm in my eighties!' "

It was obvious that they could stand around and talk about Herbie all day, and they probably would if I didn't stop them. "Which boxes are for us?" I asked.

Mom bugged her eyes at me to let me know that I was being impolite.

"Oh, right," said Darren, looking around. "It's those three over there."

He gestured at some large cartons in the corner. They were not made of air, marble, lead, or adult diapers, but they were big enough that I didn't really see how we could get them home without some kind of van. And even if we got them home, I couldn't imagine where we'd put them.

"Oh, wow," Mom said, obviously thinking the same thing I was. "This is . . . a lot of stuff! Are you sure it's all for us?"

Darren shrugged. "He wanted you to have

it. He told me, 'Everybody else I like is dead.' And you haven't even looked inside yet. Maybe it's junk. Maybe it's old newspapers."

Mom searched for a polite way to say *We don't have room for these boxes or their contents, unless they contain cash, in which case no problem—we'll just get a bigger apartment.* She came up with "This was way too generous of him. Herbie was always way too generous. Between overpaying me, and Emma's phone . . ."

Darren laughed. "Tell me about it. He left me this apartment."

Um. I wasn't sure why he was calling this four-story building an apartment, when it was practically a mansion. And I *really* didn't understand why we were standing around talking about the boxes instead of opening them and seeing what was inside. After nearly two weeks of unusually good luck, I expected to find jewelry, gold doubloons, and a genie's lamp.

I eagerly ripped the tape off the first carton

and opened it. Inside was a trove of unopened electronics, all of them in their original boxes or hard plastic packaging.

"Jackpot," I said.

I unloaded a few things onto the floor next to me so that Mom and Darren could see. It was like a technology museum in that box. Some of the things in there were so old that I didn't even know what they were supposed to do. Then there were a bunch of old iPods, old iPads, old iPhones. If it was made before 2015, and you could put an "i" in front of it, it was in that box.

Darren came over to see. He shook his head and looked up at the ceiling. "Uncle Herb, you told me you used these things all the time. You didn't even take them out of the boxes!"

Underneath the graveyard of unused gadgets were some old photo albums, thick books with plastic-covered pages full of photographs. I took one of the photo albums out and opened it carefully. The spine creaked like the door of a haunted house, and it smelled like, well, oldness.

The first page of the album had black-and-white pictures of two handsome young men in swimsuits on a beach. Something about the setting seemed familiar, or maybe it was déjà vu. The men were laughing, burying each other in the sand, posing like musclemen—generally goofing around and having fun. In the next picture, they were kissing.

"Oh, wow," said Mom, looking over my shoulder. "Herbie was so handsome."

What? I squinted at the men. I guessed the shorter one looked a little like the old man-raisin I met at the volunteer party that time. But these men were strong and healthy and they stood tall. Mom took the photo from its protective plastic and turned it over. In brown ink, with old-style penmanship, someone had written *Herb & Jack, Fire Island, 1956.*

Mom's eyes widened. "Fire Island."

Of course. That's why it looked familiar.

"You've been to Fire Island?" Darren asked, surprised. "Isn't it great? I loved visiting Uncle Herbie on Fire Island. I spent a few weeks there in the summers when I was a kid."

"My grandma has a house there," I told him.

"Really?" he asked. He smiled at Mom. "We probably crossed paths there, back in the 1980s."

I started opening the other cartons. The second box had more albums on top, which Mom started to unload. The third box had metal cans, and something that looked like a small record player. Full Stone Age technology.

"Oh, wow!" Darren looked over my shoulder at the third box. "His old filmstrips! And a slide projector, cool."

Mom's mind was a little too blown for full sentences. "But . . . I mean . . . this is . . ." She turned to Darren. "Shouldn't you have this stuff? Why did he leave these to me?"

Darren frowned. "I'm not sure. Maybe 'cause I

already have a lot of family photos? Or, you know, he did keep telling me he was going to ask 'the Computer Lady' to 'put the pictures in the computer, the way they do now.' "

"Oh!" said Mom. "Okay. He wanted the pictures scanned and digitized. Um . . ."

She was, no doubt, doing the same math I was: say one hundred pictures per album, ten albums in this box alone, that's a thousand pictures to take from the albums, scan, and replace. Plus a carton of slides. This job would take approximately two hundred years.

"You don't have to do anything with them, if you don't want to," Darren said quickly, because Darren could do math, too. "I didn't realize he was going to burden you with this, or I'd have stopped him."

"Oh, it's not a burden," Mom said. "Herbie was never a burden. If Herbie wanted his photos scanned, that's what I want to do. I'll scan them, but then I think the photo albums should be yours. I just have to figure out the most efficient way to scan so many photos at once."

Darren nodded. "Okay. Want to get something to eat while you're figuring?"

Because Mom was being agreeable, we wound up going to an Ethiopian restaurant that Darren suggested. Ethiopian food, FYI, is just piles of spicy mush, and there's no forks or spoons or knives—you're supposed to scoop up the mush with this wet, sour pancake thing and eat it like that. I took two bites and got un-hungry real quick.

I started looking at my phone, like the typical Gen Z postmillennial I am, tuning out most of their conversation. Mom and Darren talked about Herbie, North Carolina, the small party-rental business Darren co-owned, and how funny it was that they both had these ties to Fire Island. At one point when they were talking about places they'd been on Fire Island, I heard Mom say, "My friend Jenny loves that restaurant."

Loves. In the present tense. We'd been making

that mistake for two months, talking about what Aunt Jenny likes, says, wears, thinks, watches, or reads, instead of liked, said, wore, thought, watched, or read.

Mom corrected herself. "I mean, she loved it."

They decided over dinner that the smartest thing to do would be to bring Mom's scanner to Herbie's and do the scanning there, since we had no room for the boxes at our house. Meanwhile, Darren would take the old filmstrips to a place that would turn them into video files.

"I can pay whatever rate Herbie paid for your time," Darren said. "It really is asking a lot of you."

"You don't have to pay me," Mom insisted. "It won't get done quickly, but I promise it will get done. You leave tomorrow night, right? Are you comfortable with giving me a key to the apartment so I can get to work this week?"

"That would be great." Darren mopped up the last of the Ethiopian mush with the sour pancake and wiped his sticky fingers on his napkin. "I'll be back in two weeks to talk to a real estate agent about selling the place. We can meet up at Uncle Herb's, and you can show me how it's going."

Fortunately, there was no Ethiopian dessert.

After dinner, Darren insisted on walking us to the subway, even though it was only eight-thirty and the streets were full of people. "It's a Southern-gentleman thing," he said. "Besides, I need some exercise."

As though he had not been moving furniture all day before we got there.

We stood by the subway stop to say our good-byes before going down into the station.

"So . . ." said Mom.

"So . . ." said Darren.

So? I thought.

"I guess I'll see you guys two weekends from now," said Darren. He smiled a goofy smile. "Catch you then, Computer Lady. Good meeting you, Emma." He waved and walked away.

The *second* Mom and I started down the subway stairs, I asked her, "So you like him?"

"Sure," she said casually. "He's likable."

I wondered if she was being dense on purpose. "No, but do you *like him* like him?"

Mom laughed. "How would I know? I just met him! Besides, you heard him on the phone earlier. He's married, or he has a girlfriend."

Argh. Right. He and Mom got along so well, I forgot about the woman on the phone–the one who bombarded him with calls and wanted him to come home. Pauline, aka, the dealbreaker. *Who needs him?* I thought. *Him and his great-uncle's mansion and his sick abs.*

"He's short," I said. "And he has awful taste in food."

And with that the subject was dropped.

Seven

WHEN I GOT TO SCHOOL THAT MONDAY, it was obvious that Something Big had happened over the weekend. Clusters of people were standing around, exclaiming over something on their phones.

It must have involved Dakota's group, since they were the most excited. Tyler Hoff was showing off something on his phone that made the girls shriek with laughter even louder than usual. It did not sound like happy, fun laughter. It sounded evil, like a convention of Disney villains.

I walked up to Brooke, Harrison, and Geneva,

as I did every morning these days. They were clustered around Lewis, looking at his phone.

"What's going on?" I asked, trying to see what Lewis was showing everyone.

Brooke looked up at me nervously. "Um . . ." she said. "Are you sure you want to know?"

I got a bad feeling in my stomach. "Yes. Tell me. What is it?"

Lewis turned the phone my way and showed me a picture. It was Savvy. She was topless.

I literally wanted to puke.

My heart started pounding and I burst into a cold sweat. "Delete it. Delete it, Lewis. I'm serious—you have to delete it. Please. Please, Lewis."

"It's too late," he said. He gestured at the crowds of kids on the sidewalk, all looking at the picture of Savvy's exposed chest.

Oh my God. This was a nightmare. This had to be a nightmare. *Savvy is sleeping over, and for some reason I am having her nightmare.* Except I was wide awake.

I whipped my head around to see if Savvy had arrived yet. She hadn't. I wondered if she knew that her pic was going around school, and that's why she wasn't there yet. I wondered whether her moms knew and, if so, whether Ava had started skinning her alive yet. I tapped out a text to Savvy, fingers shaking.

Are you okay?

The answer, apparently, was no, because she never showed up at school. I surreptitiously checked my phone every three seconds all day, and I didn't get a reply.

By lunchtime, the teachers knew there was something going on. Everybody was too excited and distracted to pay attention in class.

Shortly before seventh period there was an announcement over the loudspeaker. "Tyler Hoff, report to Mr. Kelly's office."

The entire class went "Ooooooooooh" as Tyler packed up his book bag and left the room. He smirked like he didn't care, but I knew he was nervous from the way he looked at Lewis.

Tyler wasn't there in eighth period, and he wasn't outside after school, so nobody knew for sure what happened at the dean's office, but I assumed it wasn't good. I went to rehearsal, where I completely ignored Lewis. I wanted to squish him in my fist like an origami frog.

Afterward, I was running out of the auditorium when Lewis caught up to me.

"I'm sorry," he said. "Okay? I shouldn't have showed the picture around. But it was already out there anyway!"

I didn't want to talk to Tyler's right-hand man. "Whatever," I muttered, walking faster.

Lewis tagged along behind me. "But you have to admit, it was dumb of her to send Tyler a pic like that. It's kind of her own fault."

I turned around to face him. "It was a private picture! She's not the one who spread it everywhere! Why did he have to do that?"

Lewis threw his hands up, frustrated. "Because that's what people do! Everybody knows that!"

Okay, these are facts. We'd had a special assembly back in September to talk about online privacy, and one of the points they kept making was "Never send nudes, or everyone will see them and you will be in huge trouble." They tried to scare us by saying we could face criminal charges for having nude pictures, even of ourselves, because we're minors. I remembered how Lewis scoffed at that. Now I hoped it was true. Then I could find a policewoman and tell her, *This kid has a topless photo of an underage girl on his phone. Please lock him in the darkest cage you have for all eternity.*

He continued to follow me as I went down the stairs. "Why are you even defending Savvy?" he asked. "She doesn't care about you. When Dakota said she should stop being friends with you, she stopped. She told everybody that you liked Tyler. She showed us all your texts about him. And then she made out with him, even though she knew you liked him."

Oof. So my worst fears were true. "So what? I don't care," I said, walking faster, trying to get away from the unbearable things he said. *Savvy showed everyone my texts about Tyler?* That was even worse than her making out with him. How could she have sold me out like that? Lewis had to be lying. I was humiliated and betrayed, but I wouldn't let him see the tears in my eyes.

I was practically running from him. He stopped chasing me.

"Emma," he called after me. "I said I'm sorry!"

I ignored him and burst through the door.

I didn't notice until it was too late that Dakota, Naturi, and Sierra were waiting for me outside on the sidewalk. Suddenly, I was surrounded by the last people I wanted to see.

Dakota grabbed my arm and got right in my face. "You told on Tyler," she growled. "Now you're going to pay for it."

"I didn't tell!" The words came out squeaky. "I didn't, I swear!"

Naturi chimed in. "Who else would do it? Who else would take Savvy's side? She has no friends but you."

"You're in so much trouble," said Sierra.

Dakota smiled. "We're going to make your life hell."

Already done, I thought.

Melanie the Playwright came out the front door, wearing her earbuds and frowning at something on her phone, until she saw me surrounded by the mean girls. Dakota dropped my arm and put on a fake smile as Melanie approached.

"Hey, Emma," said Melanie, ignoring everyone else. "You ready to go get a latte with me?"

"Yep." I wiggled away from my tormentors. They looked at me with narrowed eyes. They weren't able to get me today, but they wouldn't stop trying until they did.

Melanie and I walked side by side in silence for

a block. I tried to get my heart to calm down, but I felt really shaky. I was going to thank her for stepping in like that, but she started talking like everything was normal.

"I think we're in good shape for the show, if Carter ever learns his lines. I mean, at least he's trying . . ."

I wasn't listening. I was trying to comprehend the events of the day and what they meant. If Savvy really showed everyone my texts, she'd betrayed me more than I could have ever imagined. But then her new friends betrayed her even worse. I couldn't help feeling protective of her. Maybe it was habit, built up over five years of best friendship, or maybe it was my incredible Penguin-level degree of loyalty, but even after what Savvy did to me, my anger was nothing compared to how bad I felt for her.

Melanie continued her monologue. "And I thought about expanding the Julian character, but I'll have to save that for another version . . ."

I also felt terrible for myself now that Dakota's group was officially out to get me for supposedly ratting on Tyler. So unfair! I didn't even get the joy of ratting on him, and I was taking the punishment for it. But maybe if I could find out who really snitched, they'd leave me alone.

"I thought Ms. Engel was crazy when she suggested Lewis, but he's not half-bad, lucky for us . . ."

I bit my tongue so I wouldn't say what I was thinking: the words "luck" and "Lewis" did not belong in the same sentence, unless "luck" was attached to the words "horrible," "miserable," or "worst ever possible."

Melanie and I reached the coffee place. I didn't want anything, so I got us a table. At the counter, she ordered some very complicated coffee drink, with a lot of extra instructions: "And can you make the milk very hot, please? And can I get cinnamon on top, but just two shakes . . ."

The beverage was produced, and she carried it

to the table. "So," she said to me as she sat. "What was up with your friends back there?"

I cringed. "It's nothing. They just hate me."

"Why?"

It had been a while since I had someone to talk with about this kind of stuff, so I wound up telling Melanie the whole story about Savvy: how she'd been hot and cold to me for the last few weeks, how she hung out with the devil and hooked up with my crush. It was a relief to get it all out.

Eventually, I got to today—the topless pic and Tyler's punishment. "So now they all think I snitched on Tyler," I said. "And I didn't. I almost wish I did, since they hate me for it anyway."

Melanie nodded with understanding. "I know a few things about being hated," she said.

"Yeah?" I was surprised. Melanie had plenty of friends, as far as I could see, and now she was an award-winning playwright. Who wouldn't want to be friends with Melanie?

"Sure," she confirmed. "And eighth grade was the worst. You know why I wear all black? Because my hope for the human race died in eighth grade. That's when my 'best friends' told me I should kill myself because I was so depressing. They said everyone would be happier because nobody wanted me around."

Melanie was either reading my texts or reading my mind. "That's like, almost exactly what they said to me."

"Yeah, well. That was three years ago. And I just found out last week that one of my old 'best friends' is in the hospital with anorexia. And what's strange is, I wished for so many bad things to happen to her, but when I heard that something bad *did* happen, I felt really sad for her, and I wished it hadn't happened."

"Why were you sad for her?" I could picture Dakota starving herself to death and me being totally cheerful about it.

"Because her karma sucks."

Karma? I remembered Aunt Jenny using that word a few times. The way she'd explained it to me was, "It means everything that comes around, goes around." But I wasn't fully clear on it, so I just nodded.

Melanie took a sip of her latte and continued. "I mean, look what happens. People are mean to me, so I stay home and write. They're all hanging out, posting pictures, and I'm miserable and alone. I write all the time, and my writing gets better. Then I win an award for writing. Then the school decides to produce my play. And next year, I'm going to have a good shot at a full college scholarship, all because of a play I would never have written if those girls hadn't been such bitches."

This was exactly what I was starting to notice: how everything was related, how the bad things that happened sometimes led to good things later. Melanie's story of triumph almost gave me a ray of hope, until I remembered how messed up everything was.

"So I'm grateful to those girls," Melanie continued. "And now they have to watch me succeed, which is the worst thing I could possibly do to them."

"Like the motto," I said. "Living well is the best revenge."

"Exactly! I felt jealous of those girls, and now they feel jealous of me. So we're even! But one of them is suffering from anorexia, and that's horrible."

I understood. No matter how upset I was at Savvy, I never wanted her to be used and humiliated that way.

I thanked Melanie for the talk, and for saving me from those girls on the sidewalk. Then I walked slowly the rest of the way home. I wasn't going to tell Mom what happened with Savvy's picture—I knew she'd give me a huge lecture about safety and privacy, call Savvy's moms, and make everything worse. Fortunately, Mom was on the phone when I got home.

I closed my door, sat on my bed, and pulled out my luck list, which I'd hidden under a bunch of papers for school. The list was covered in changes and checkmarks and things I'd crossed off.

What if I tried to use my luck to help Savvy somehow? She was already being punished for fooling around with Tyler. And now she didn't have a single friend on her side. I knew what that felt like. Later, after she was out of this mess, she could tell me she was sorry for getting caught up in the social game—and I'd tell her how much she hurt me, but I'd forgive her. And then, decades into the future, we could tell our daughters the story of how we almost fought over a guy.

There was no way for me to help her without some superhuman luck. Even *with* superhuman luck it was a long shot. But it wouldn't hurt to try.

I scratched out item number 8:

~~8. Mom forgets my upcoming dentist appointment.~~

Then I wrote:

8. Help Savvy.

I had just put the list back in its hiding place when Mom ended her call and poked her head into my room.

"Bloop."

"Bloop."

"How was your day?" she asked.

"Okay. Rehearsal was frustrating. Carter still doesn't know his lines."

"Good thing I know all of them," Mom said. It was true–in the process of helping me learn my lines, she had memorized the father's part. "If they need an understudy, tell them I'd be happy to step in."

I smiled, but I wasn't doing a great job of acting like nothing was wrong. I still needed to get out of her face for a few minutes and get myself straight. "I better walk Penguin," I said, sliding off my bed.

"Thanks, Bloop."

I put on his leash and grabbed my coat. I was halfway out the door when Mom stopped me.

"Oh, hey, I forgot. You have an appointment with the dentist next Thursday, so you might have to leave rehearsal early."

Damn, I thought as the door swung closed behind me. *That was fast.*

✉

The week wore on, and Savvy did not come back to school. She didn't answer texts, she didn't answer emails, her Instagram and Snapchat were gone. She must have been super-mega-extra-fully-forever grounded. Tyler had been suspended from school for the week, which was good, because I never wanted to see his face again.

Since I couldn't reach Savvy any other way, I decided to go by her apartment and slide a note under her door, just a few lines to let her know that I was still on her side. A letter slid under my door had brought good things—maybe my note would do the same for her.

I went by her building after rehearsal on Friday. Someone came out of the building and held the door for me to enter.

I climbed the stairs with their familiar musty smell. Savvy and I used to run up and down those stairs together all the time, but it had been months since I'd been there. It made me feel nostalgic for our old friendship. So I decided that, rather than slip the note under the door, I'd knock and see if she was home.

Savvy's mom Charise answered my knock. She was surprised to see me.

"Hey, Emma." Charise did not invite me inside, but I could smell something delicious coming from the kitchen, as usual—she was a private chef and was probably making a dessert for one of her clients. She stood in the doorway and folded her arms over her apron. "Savvy is not allowed to see her friends right now."

"Sorry for stopping by," I said. I handed her the note. "Can you please give this to her? I just wanted to tell her I hope she's okay."

Charise looked me dead in the eye as she unfolded my note. Then she read it aloud:

Dear Savvy,

I'm so so so so sorry that Tyler turned out to be such a terrible person. You didn't deserve what he did to you. Even though we haven't been close these past few weeks, I still think of you as my best friend.

Love, Emma

Charise considered the note, considered me, and made a decision. "Come in," she said. "You get two minutes."

Savvy was on the couch, reading a book. When

she saw me, she ducked her head and started to cry. I ran over to give her a hug, then sat down beside her.

"I'm sorry," she said. "Emma, I'm so sorry I was mean to you. I never should have been friends with those guys—"

"It's okay," I told her. Now I was crying, too. "All I care about is how you are."

She sniffled and wiped her nose with her sleeve. "I can't believe Tyler did this to me."

I could. That's the thing about super-good-looking guys—they can do whatever they want, and nobody says no to them. Not even adults.

"He's the worst person in the world," I said. "He should die a slow and painful death."

Savvy nodded ruefully. "He kept begging me to send him a pic. I said no, but he said the others wouldn't want me around if I was going to be a little baby. Dakota and Sierra told me everybody does it—they said they send pics to guys all the time. So I sent him a Snap. And then he sent the screenshot to all his friends." She started ugly-crying again.

I felt so helpless. I would have done anything to make things better for Savvy, but there was nothing I could do. My friend was suffering, and I couldn't do anything to help her. This must have been how Mom felt when Aunt Jenny got sick.

Charise watched us with folded arms. "All right," she said. "Time's up."

I gave Savvy another hug. "I'll come see you again soon," I whispered.

She squeezed me, so I knew she heard.

I let Charise escort me back to the apartment door. "Thank you for letting me come in," I said.

She nodded. "Next time, I won't. I know you weren't a part of this. But she's punished for the rest of the school year, and that means no visitors."

"When does she get to come back to school?" I asked.

Charise raised her voice so it could be heard in

the living room. "Savannah doesn't get to go back to school."

I didn't understand. Of course she'd go back to school. Everybody had to go to school. It was the law. Her moms couldn't punish her by keeping her home forever, could they?

"What do you mean?" I asked.

"I mean," said Charise, "that Savannah's not going back to Knights, or going to any other school. She's being homeschooled from now on."

Then she closed the door in my face.

Eight

THAT WEEKEND, THE THIRD IN MY LUCKY month, we went to Grandma's beach house on Fire Island. It was a three-hour trip that involved a subway, two trains, a van, and a ferry. Last time we made the trek, Aunt Jenny was with us, so it didn't feel like three hours. Time flew by when she was around.

I closed my eyes as the ferry carried us to the island. I could hear last year's conversation so clearly. Aunt Jenny and Mom were talking about how hard it was to find a boyfriend at their age.

"The good ones are already married," Mom said.

Aunt Jenny nodded. “Even the bad ones are married.”

They laughed. I knew she was talking about their friend Casey and her horrible husband, Ken, so I laughed, too.

“I still have hope, though,” Aunt Jenny continued. “My horoscope this week was ‘Tell the universe what you want, and it will echo it back to you.’ Isn’t that cool?”

I shrugged. Sounded like mumbo jumbo to me. But if it worked for Aunt Jenny, it was cool.

She continued. “So yesterday I sat down and made a list of things I wanted in a boyfriend. Like, he has to have a job. He doesn’t have to love the job. But he can’t hate the job. I don’t want to be with someone who’s miserable every day.”

“You’re asking a lot,” Mom said, laughing. “I think I’d be happy with just the job part.”

“Well, you have to be very specific with the universe,” Aunt Jenny said. “You have to let it know exactly what you’re looking for. And part of that is sitting down and deciding, 'These are the things I want.' You have to pick a destination; otherwise you'll spend all your time going in circles."

I snapped back to the present. Aunt Jenny was gone. She would never reach her destination or find that perfect boyfriend who fit everything on her list. *The universe was a jerk.*

When we stepped off the boat, Grandma was waving at us from the dock. She greeted us with lipstick-y kisses that smelled like gin. I saw Mom stiffen a little bit, but she smiled and told Grandma how happy we were to see her.

"Wait until you see the house. The whole front of the deck needs to be powerwashed. You know, I got the Luss boy—what's his name, Carl? I got him to do it for me last year for fifteen dollars, but this year he wants double. Can you imagine? I said, 'You need double what you got last year? Did they raise the price of water?' And he says to me . . ."

Grandma's complaints lasted the whole

ten-minute walk to her house, and they didn't stop there.

"I told him at the market, 'I'm not buying your rotten lettuce anymore.' Last three times I bought lettuce, it was slimy on the bottom, but they put a piece of paper towel in there so you can't see."

In a way, it was good that Grandma talked about nothing all the time. It was like having a TV on in the background. We didn't have to have any difficult conversations or talk about painful memories. Mom leafed through magazines and stared at the ocean and said "Uh-huh" every so often. I made popcorn on the stove the old-fashioned way and said "Uh-huh" whenever Mom did.

Everything in the city—school, the show, Savvy, and Dakota and her crew—seemed very far away. And since Grandma never asks anybody else how they're doing, I didn't have to talk about any of it.

"I'm gonna go see who's around," I said.

"Okay," said Mom. "Have fun."

"Don't go too far," said Grandma. "And if you stop by the market while you're out, see if they have any decent produce or if it's all garbage. It's outrageous, what they try to get away with, with the prices they charge . . ."

I let the door swing closed after me and walked around town aimlessly. It wouldn't be beach weather for a few months–it was May, but it was chilly and windy out, and there weren't many people around. I put the hood of my sweatshirt up and headed for the water.

The wind on the beach was fierce. Walking into it was a struggle. The waves were gray and foamy, and they sprayed mist along the shore. I was cold and wet, and the wind blew at me hard, but I kept going.

I am an Antarctic explorer, I told myself. *I must reach the base camp before the sun goes down or I'll die.*

There was somebody farther down the beach

looking for shells. *This person is my only hope,* I thought. *I must catch up to this person or I'll die.*

I wasn't actually going to fling myself at whoever it was and beg them to save me from the crippling cold. It was just a game to play with myself, to keep my legs moving and my brain occupied. I got closer and closer to my mystery savior, and realized it was Bobby Dudderman, who I'd known since we were both six years old. Us kids all called him Bobby the Dud.

Bobby was looking intently at the rocks and shells on the ground. He had been collecting stuff from the beach forever. His pockets were always ripped from carrying things around. He showed no interest in playing games, or socializing in general. If his parents hadn't forced him to go to other kids' parties, we probably wouldn't even have known his name.

He looked up as I approached. He had grown two inches and gotten a super-short haircut since I last saw him. It was weird how different it made him look.

“Hey,” I said.

“Hey,” he said, and went back to looking at the sand.

I passed him and kept walking for a while, then sat down on a washed-up log. Bobby moved slowly and deliberately down the beach. I envied him. He didn’t need other people. He was perfectly happy being himself, by himself. He would never know the pain of losing a friend, the way Mom and I did.

I stared at the ocean. I was thinking about my luck. There were ten days left in my lucky month, and then . . . And then what? Would I go back to being unlucky? Would every good thing that had happened be undone? Would I lose my phone and screw up the play and make more people hate me? How was this supposed to work?

I didn’t even know if I’d get an explanation for the letter and who sent it, or if I’d just have to go on wondering forever. It was so frustrating.

I wrapped my arms around my knees and

squeezed my eyes shut tight. When I looked up, Bobby was walking toward me with his hand outstretched.

"Here."

He gave me something small, smooth, and blue. It was warm from his hand, and it curved to fit perfectly into my palm. "Cool."

"Beach glass is hard to find now. It used to be ubiquitous, but the advent of plastic bottles caused a paucity."

And he was off, talking about something science-y. It didn't matter to him whether I understood or not. He just enjoyed discussing the things he loved. Sometimes he could sound like a computer, but as he told me about the "ramifications of the plasticization of the oceans," he seemed excited and alive.

I suddenly realized that Bobby was the perfect person to talk to about the letter. He knew about a lot of hard-to-explain things—maybe he could help explain this to me. I knew he wouldn't look at me like I was nuts if I told him something crazy, and he certainly wouldn't tell anybody else. The letter said I should tell "no human person," but Bobby was the most robotic person I knew. And the month was more than half over anyway.

I decided to risk it.

"What do you know about luck?" I asked.

The fact that I totally switched the subject with no warning did not bother Bobby. He was squatting on the sand, emptying his pockets and surveying his finds. "You mean mathematical probability? I have a superficial understanding of the mechanics. Why?"

"I don't know. Weird things have been happening, and I don't know what's going on."

Bobby started to sort his treasures on the sand: scallop shells over here, smooth ones over there; round pebbles over here, chunky rocks over there. Every so often he picked up an item and chucked it over his shoulder. "That's the definition of life," he said without looking up.

"Okay, right. But about three weeks ago, I got this letter . . ."

I told him the whole story: the letter, the list, the way some of the things on the list had come true and some had gone bad. I was aware of how kooky it sounded, but it was such a relief to talk about it, finally, to say the words out loud. If that meant my luck would end, I'd have to live with that, because I couldn't live with a secret this big for much longer.

When I finished my story, Bobby nodded. He thought for a minute, then nodded again.

"The letter was written by human hand," he said.

"Well, typed by a human on a computer. There was no handwriting, so I couldn't tell if it was someone I knew."

"But the letter was composed and delivered by a human. The words were not put on paper by a deity or a magical being."

"Well, I mean, obviously . . ."

I said "obviously," but this had not been a hundred percent obvious to me until Bobby said it. I mean, science doesn't explain *everything* about the way the world works. Maybe there was some kindly wizard or good fairy or magic angel looking out for me. But, of course, Bobby was right. It was just a plain old person.

Bobby continued. "Humans don't have the power to see or influence the future. Studies of psychic ability have not found a reliable correlation between predictions and outcomes."

The look on my face must have said *Huh?* because Bobby rephrased his sentence.

"Psychics aren't real."

"Oh, right."

Aunt Jenny went to see a psychic last October, right around her diagnosis. The psychic told her she would make a full recovery, and charged her a hundred bucks. I wanted to find that psychic and stomp on all the little bones in her foot and take Aunt Jenny's money back.

"So you think it's a hoax?" I asked. "Somebody messing with me?"

Bobby didn't say anything.

"I mean, of course it's a hoax. Nobody can control someone else's luck."

Still quiet.

"Even though there's been a lot of coincidences lately. They're just coincidences."

Bobby finally spoke. "If you believe in it, then it works."

I wasn't sure what he meant. "What, like Tinkerbell?"

"No. Like the placebo effect."

I gave him another blank look.

"It's a scientific phenomenon. A placebo is a fake pill. In headache studies, for example, researchers tell the test participants they're being given aspirin for their headache. But what some of the participants are really getting is a fake pill with no medicine in it. Often, the participants who take the placebo find that their headache is cured anyway. The participants expect the pill to work, so it does. Someone told you that you would be lucky this month, and so you are. Or so you perceive."

I tried to understand what Bobby was telling me. "So it's a fake-out?"

"It depends," he said. He rose to his feet and made eye contact for the first time since we'd been talking. "Is your headache cured?"

"I'm not sure," I said.

Bobby resumed scanning the beach for treasure. "Then maybe it wasn't hurting in the first place," he said, walking away.

✉

I was just as confused after talking with Bobby as I had been before. I walked back to the house, stopping outside to shake the sand off my feet so Grandma wouldn't complain about me getting sand in her beach house, which, btw, is *built on sand*. Then I heard Mom's voice.

"The school suspended the boy for a week," she said. "And they suspended Savannah, too, even though she's the victim. Like the poor girl hasn't been punished enough! It's so backward and sexist, but nowadays all the schools have these zero-tolerance policies when it comes to sending those pictures. Those kids are lucky they weren't expelled."

Grandma clucked. "They *should* expel them! You don't want Emma going to school with kids like that."

"Oh, give me a break," said Mom. "We've known Savvy since she was eight years old. She's a normal girl who made a common mistake. Savvy wanted to be popular, and she got peer-pressured. It could've just as easily been Emma, falling for that boy. She's lucky she wasn't 'cool' enough to hang out with the popular kids."

I froze.

As much as it sucked to hear it said out loud, casually, like a fact everybody accepted about the world, I knew Mom was right: My fundamental lack of coolness probably saved me. If the popular group had ever liked me—if I'd gotten everything I put on my luck list—*I* would have been the one hanging out at Dakota's. *I* would have been the one making out with Tyler Hoff. *Me.* Not Savvy. And *I* would have done anything Tyler asked of me—even send him a topless pic.

Luck, I was starting to realize, comes in many flavors. I'd been thinking of luck as "things I wanted to happen," but luck was also "preventing things I *didn't* want to happen." I had been lucky all afternoon—lucky a rogue wave didn't sweep me out to sea, lucky I didn't trip on the boardwalk and break my back, lucky that it was Bobby on the deserted beach and not a serial killer. Something bad could have happened to me, but it didn't.

It happened to Savvy instead.

I finished de-sanding myself and went inside. Mom and Grandma killed their conversation as soon as I opened the door.

"Bloop," said Mom.

"Where did you go?" asked Grandma. She sounded suspicious, as if maybe instead of walking on the beach I'd been out sending topless pics of myself to the world at large.

"Beach," I said. Before she could say it, I added, "Don't worry—I shook off the sand."

✉

That afternoon, Mom went to the island's one daily AA meeting. Grandma "rested her eyes for a minute," which means she "fell asleep snoring on the couch for two hours."

I read and did schoolwork and looked at my phone for a while. Waggytail had posted pics of the new dogs for adoption, and I hearted them all. Brooke had pics of her and Harrison trying on costumes at the costume shop: Harrison as an Egyptian king, Brooke as a pirate, the two of them wearing the two halves of a bear costume. The head of the bear looked hilarious with Harrison's skinny legs sticking out, and Brooke looked like she was wearing giant furry overalls made for a huge fat man. Heart, heart, heart, crying-from-laughing emoji, *stop having fun without me*, LOL.

Venice Biandi had also posted some pics of herself at Dakota's house, looking like she'd climbed up another step on the social ladder. There she was, doing duckface with Dakota and Naturi, draped seductively across Tyler's lap.

Careful, Venice, I thought. *Keep that shirt on.*

When Mom came back, Grandma was still asleep. "Let's go down to the bay and watch the sunset," Mom suggested. I grabbed my hoodie, put on Penguin's leash, and followed her.

I could feel Aunt Jenny walking beside us. Early in the season, when the horseshoe crabs would crawl onto the shore to mate, Aunt Jenny would go down to the bay and look for any that were stuck on their backs in the sand. Once they're beached like that, they're basically food for the seagulls. It's pretty gruesome. Aunt Jenny would take a beached crab and pick it up by the sides of its shell and chuck it back into the bay, saving its life.

"No need to thank me," she'd call as the crab scooted away into deeper water. "Live your life to the fullest—that's thanks enough for me."

I always thought it was kind of silly. Once when we were crab hunting and I'd grown bored of it, I told her it was dumb. "It'll just wash up and get beached again. You can't save them all."

Aunt Jenny picked up a big old crusty crab. It waved its claws at me. "But I can save this one."

Now I wondered how many crabs Aunt Jenny saved, and how many babies those crabs had. This summer, she would save none. If a crab got beached, it was getting eaten alive by a bird. *Bad luck for you, crab.*

Mom must have been thinking the same thing. "I bet the crabs are sad Aunt Jenny's not coming this year."

"Yeah. It's gonna be a crab-pocalypse."

"Yeah. Unless . . ."

"Unless what?" I asked, uneasy. There was no way I could pick up one of those creepy-crawly things with all the legs and whatnot. Even if it meant that I was dooming the creatures to a gory death. I. Just. Could. Not.

"We could get a shovel," Mom said, stopping short. "Let's go back and get the shovel."

We headed back to the house, got the shovel, and hurried over to the bay, where six or seven crabs were stuck on their backs. Mom used the shovel to scoop them up and deposit them into the water. The seagulls squawked and cried, clearly yelling in seagull-ese, "YOU STUPID JERKS JUST RUINED DINNER." Penguin barked at them until they fled.

We sat where the ground met the dune, where the sand was dry and the bugs weren't too bad. The sun was thinking about going down, but it hadn't made up its mind yet. It hung over the bay, making everything brilliant and pink and orange, then sank gradually, like a kid who's tired but doesn't want to fall asleep.

Aunt Jenny was gone. But the crabs were saved.

"Bloop," said Mom.

"Bloop," I confirmed.

"Wrff," added Penguin. We took our shovel and walked home.

✉

We'd just made it back to our apartment on Sunday evening, after the epic return journey from Grandma's, and we were scouring the fridge for something quick to make for dinner when Mom got a FaceTime request from Darren.

I thought she'd ignore it, but she smoothed her hair and straightened her shirt and sat down to answer it on her laptop. "Hey, Dare," she said brightly when the connection came through. "What's up?"

Dare? I thought.

"Hey, Katie the Computer Lady."

Mom laughed. I froze. *OMG.* They were *flirting.* So, so awkward. Few things are as cringeworthy as witnessing your parent flirt. It's like accidentally walking into the bathroom while they're pooping. Nobody wants to see that.

More important, Mom's not allowed to flirt with men who have wives or girlfriends. This is the rule her best friend made right after Mom became unintentionally pregnant by a married man. Aunt Jenny agreed with Mom that, yes, it all worked out for the best, because I was the greatest thing that ever happened to her and to the universe in general. But Mom had to agree with Aunt Jenny that she could have picked an *un*married man to get *intentionally* pregnant with, instead of the other way around.

Then, two years ago, there was a client named Pete who told Mom he wanted to leave his wife so he could be with her, even though he and Mom had never even kissed. I wouldn't have known anything about that situation, but Mom and Aunt Jenny were talking about it one night in the kitchen when I happened to be in an eavesdropping mood.

"I'm not trying to break up a marriage!" Mom said to Aunt Jenny. "It's not my fault Pete went nuts. I never said I wanted to be romantic with him. I don't know where he got that idea, but it wasn't from me!"

Aunt Jenny could raise one eyebrow without the other one, something she was often forced to do with Mom. I didn't hear Mom say anything in reply, so I assumed Aunt Jenny had deployed the eyebrow.

"Okay," Mom confessed. "I flirted with him. But he started it! And there was no physical contact!" Pause. "And I already quit working for him! I'm never going to see him again."

Another silence. Aunt Jenny's eyebrow must have been working overtime.

"Fine," said Mom. "I solemnly swear that I will

never again flirt with a man who's in a relationship. Okay?"

And now, here she was sitting in the exact same chair in the exact same kitchen where she swore to Aunt Jenny that she would never again flirt with a taken guy. Flirting with a taken guy.

"Hey," I said loudly. "Your child is starving to death."

She looked at me like *You better hurry up and die, then, before I kill you.*

I didn't know if she knew what I was thinking or why I was being a brat. But she did end the call and close the laptop, and we skipped the cooking and went out to the diner down the block.

And that, I sincerely hoped, was the end of that.

Nine

"HEY, RAT. WANT SOME CHEESE?"

It was Lucky Day 22. Dakota stood in front of my lunch table, arms folded. Brooke, Harrison, Geneva, and the rest of the cast acted like they weren't there. We were pretty great at it, because we're actors. If we ran out of conversation, we just said our lines from the show, with the word "banana" in place of the nouns ("You're my whole banana!" "But I need my own banana!" "If your banana was still alive, she'd agree with me." Etc.).

Naturi sneered at me. "Or are you having garbage for lunch?"

My drama friends had become my buffer at school, keeping me safe from the whispers and looks people hurled at me. It wasn't just Dakota's group that was bugging me; it was most of the kids in the eighth grade. Every kid knows you're not supposed to tattle to adults, and even people who weren't friends with Tyler hated me for ratting on him.

Which, as you will recall, I did not do.

Tyler returned to school as popular as ever: a hero to the boys, a magnet to the girls. Meanwhile, Savvy had become a fictional character. People felt free to make up stories about things she supposedly did. All they had to do was start a sentence with "I heard she . . ." and then they could say anything they liked. Over the course of five days, I'd heard that (1) Savvy was in love with Tyler and wouldn't stop texting him, (2) Savvy was a sexting addict, and (3) Savvy was pregnant.

"Rat!" Sierra said sharply. "Why aren't you squealing?"

I wouldn't give Dakota and her crew the satisfaction of a response. They couldn't get to me. They could taunt me at lunch, but I was surrounded by supportive friends. They could catch up to me in the girls' locker room after gym, but . . .

But nothing, actually. That was legit scary. Nobody else was there, and Dakota had me backed up against a locker, with the combination lock sticking into my back.

"You messed with Tyler," she growled at me. "*Nobody* messes with my friend."

I didn't mess with Tyler! I wanted to say, but not a lot of air was reaching my brain at that moment. Dakota's hot breath was right in my face, and her fist was ready to follow.

Just as I was mentally writing my will, the janitor yelled from the hallway. "Time to go, ladies. I gotta mop up in there."

Gratefully, I scooted past them and ran to math class.

This was my life.

Don't get me wrong—there were some bright spots, namely, everything having to do with the play. Me and Brooke and Harrison and Geneva—or some combination thereof—were together so much, we'd developed a shorthand code that involved us saying things like "That's not your mustard" or "Jabberwocky makes sense now," to the total bafflement of everyone around us.

Also, I really enjoyed acting. It turned out that I could cry on cue by thinking of Mom crying after Aunt Jenny's funeral, which was the saddest sight I'd ever seen. Ms. Engel was full of praise for me, and Melanie said I fully embodied Nadine. "You brought her to life," she said dramatically (of course). When I was at rehearsal, I felt great.

Except for one thing: Lewis.

I hated him with the fire of a thousand burning suns. He had helped spread the picture of Savvy. He hung out with the worst human beings on the planet. He did nothing while his friends harassed me in the lunchroom and any other room they could catch me in. He sat at the cool table with a smirky smile on his face, and I would have given up a kidney if I could have slapped him hard enough to wipe it off permanently.

✉

"Today," said Ms. Engel at Wednesday afternoon's rehearsal, "we rehearse the love scene."

Of course.

Lewis's smirk twisted into something else. He took his position on the stage and waited for me. I dragged my feet, dreading every second of this.

"Let's start where Julian enters," said Ms. Engel. "From 'Psst, Nadine, over here!' Okay?"

Lewis climbed the stepladder representing the tree outside Nadine's window. The crew was building a great-looking fake tree, but it wasn't done yet. Most of the crew members were upper schoolers, and a few of the guys were severely hot. Another bonus of the theatrical life.

"'Psst, Nadine,'" said Lewis, knocking on an invisible pane of glass. "'Over here!'"

I couldn't look him in the eyes. I wished this were a scene where I had to get really angry, because I could have done that with no problem. Instead, it was a tender scene in which Julian tells Nadine that he won't let her father come between them.

"Okay, Emma," said Ms. Engel. "You're over by the dresser brushing your hair."

I stood downstage left and mimed brushing.

"Then you hear him, and you stop, but you don't turn. Remember, you're hoping he will go away on his own, so you don't have to feel stuck between him and your father."

Hoping he will go away. That I could do. All through the scene, as Lewis climbed down off the ladder and we said our lines standing close to each other, I stared at his chin instead of his eyes and thought, *Go away, go away, go away.*

At one point Ms. Engel said, "Okay, maybe less

resistance to him, Emma. Yes, you're trying to be strong, but this is the man you love. Also, eye contact. I feel like you're not connecting somehow."

I looked into Lewis's eyes. I hadn't really done that before. He was usually squinting or looking down his nose at people. Now his eyes were wide open. Lewis's eyes were hazel and green, with stubby brown lashes, and they looked . . . sad.

In my mind, I'd been saying, *Go away, go away, go away.* I knew he heard me loud and clear. I didn't know for sure what Lewis was thinking, but his eyes said, *I'm sorry, I'm sorry, I'm sorry.*

No you're not.

He reached for my hand, as instructed by the script. He held it gently in his own, caressing it with his thumb.

"I love that thumb thing," said Ms. Engel. "Even if they can't see it past the first three rows. Perfect. Emma, keep looking into his eyes."

Yes, I am. I'm sorry. Please believe me.

No. Drop dead.

"Okay," Ms. Engel said. "Now you lean forward . . ."

Lewis leaned forward.

"And you kiss her."

Lewis gave me one last searching look. *Please, Emma, don't hate me.*

I thought you loved being hated.

Not by you.

He touched my face with his fingers, closed his eyes, and then his warm lips met mine. He kissed me softly, not too much pressure—a teasing, tingling kiss. My head spun, and my disloyal, idiot lips were like "YES. THIS. MORE." Lewis slowly withdrew and looked at me.

"Wow," said Ms. Engel.

"Wow," said Melanie.

WOW, I thought. My pulse was pounding. *Why?* I'd kissed boys before, playing spin-the-bottle and stuff, nothing very romantic. But I had never really been kissed by a boy. Not like that.

I looked at Lewis, alarmed. He had dropped

to one knee and was retying his shoe. It almost looked like he was going to propose.

He looked up at me with concern. *Was that okay? I know you didn't want to kiss me, but it was in the script.*

I tried to catch my breath and steady my gaze. *Yeah, that was okay.*

Lewis smiled. Not smirked, not leered, but smiled. I couldn't help it—I smiled back at him.

"Guys, that was great," said Ms. Engel. "Now let's take it from the top again."

✉

There was less than a week left in my supposedly lucky month.

I hadn't been paying much attention to the letter or my list, not since Bobby Dudderman had told me it was probably bogus. I stopped over-thinking every little good thing that happened to me—every postponed exam, every bus I caught at the last second, every time Mom was in a ridiculously good mood for seemingly no reason at all. These were all normal, everyday things that would have happened with or without the letter.

I was tired of getting excited every time someone mentioned luck, tired of analyzing every chain of events—this happened, which caused that to happen, and then that led to the other thing. Everything that happened had been a coincidence. Sure, there'd been a lot of coincidences since I got the letter, but that, too, was just another coincidence. I decided to ignore the stupid letter. It wasn't real.

Then I got the second one.

Are you kidding me? I thought when I walked into the kitchen that Wednesday morning and saw the envelope on the floor. Mom was still asleep, or maybe she was pretending to be asleep. Either way, it sure was a *coincidence* that she was sleeping late the day the second note was delivered.

I grabbed the envelope, ripped it open, and pulled out the letter. There were only two words on it. They were:

It's real.

I spun around. This had to be a hidden-camera situation. I waved at the ceiling, thinking that's where the cameras probably were, and muttered, "I'm onto you guys. I know it's a joke, so you can stop now."

The ceiling looked back at me blankly.

I was definitely going crazy.

Just as I'd been thinking the letter was fake, the letter writer read my mind, wrote another letter, and delivered it on a morning when Mom happened to be asleep. *Explain that, Bobby the Dud. Show me the science behind that.* Maybe wizards or fairies or angels really did exist after all. "Placebo effect" my butt.

I took Penguin for his walk, stopping at a

bench near the dog park so I could analyze the new letter. It was delivered in the same kind of envelope as the first one—white, and squarer and smaller than your average envelope—and the paper was once again regular printer paper. I scoured it for more clues: a hair stuck to the glue on the envelope, or a stray fiber from someone's coat. It was always a hair or a fiber that revealed the killer on those crime shows. But all I saw were the two words:

It's real.

I held the paper to my nose. It smelled a little like cigarette smoke, but so did everything in the hallway. I held it up to the light to see if that made a difference, and that's how I saw it. A tiny yellow stain at the very bottom edge on the back of the page. And who did I know with stained yellow fingers?

Fran.

That sneaky, sneaky superintendent! After our chat, I'd eliminated her as a suspect. Now, the more I thought about it, the more it seemed clear that the letters had come from Fran. Nobody else had the opportunity to slip things under my door, and here was her signature yellow stain. It had to be her. But why? I still couldn't come up with a motive for her to leave me these strange letters, but at least now I had an actual, physical clue.

I was so busy analyzing the stain on the letter, I didn't notice that Penguin was chomping on a chicken bone until I heard him making a choking noise.

"PENGUIN!"

I grabbed him and tried to pry his mouth open, but I wasn't strong enough. Penguin was making the worst sounds I'd ever heard. He couldn't breathe, and I couldn't do anything about it.

"Help!" I yelled, freaking out. "He's choking!"

A man in a red plaid lumberjack shirt ran over.

"Let me," he said, straddling Penguin on the

ground. He put his hands around Penguin's rib cage and made a thrusting motion. Penguin's eyes bugged out and he tried to wiggle away, but the man did it again, and a sliver of chicken bone popped out of Penguin's mouth onto the ground.

Penguin looked up at the man gratefully and panted like he'd just run a doggie marathon. "Wrff," he said, and sneezed.

I had never been so happy to hear my dog sneeze.

I started sobbing with relief. "Thank you," I cried to the lumberjack man. "Thank you so much, thank you so much. If you hadn't been there . . ."

"He's okay, though. Everything's okay." He looked at me with kind eyes, and his voice was reassuring. "I'm glad I could help."

I collapsed onto the bench, hugging Penguin and weeping into his fur. My whole body trembled. If Penguin had died, it would have been my fault, and I never would have forgiven myself.

There was no way my legs were going to carry me home. The day had already been fully bananas, and it wasn't even eight o'clock. I called Mom.

She sounded fuzzy, until she heard me crying. Then she snapped into problem-solving mode. "What is it? What's happening?"

I couldn't catch my breath. My words came out in a stutter. "P-Penguin . . . a bone . . . he c-couldn't . . ."

Mom didn't understand me and started freaking out. "Oh no! Oh, no, baby, not Penguin . . ."

"No, he's . . . There was a man . . ."

The nice lumberjack gently took the phone from my hand. "Hi there. Your dog is fine. He was choking, but we managed to get the bone out of his throat. Your daughter is hugging him right now."

I could hear Mom's cry of relief. "Thank you! I can't thank you enough! Oh, God, thank you!"

"I'm glad I could help," the man said, and handed me my phone.

"I'm coming," said Mom. "Where are you?"

I described the location of the bench between sobs.

"Stay put. I'll be right there."

I hung up. Penguin's savior sat down on the bench next to me. "I'm Conrad," he said.

"I'm Emma," I tried to say, but it sounded more like *amammama*.

"I like your dog's name. Did you come up with it?"

I nodded.

"My dog was named Fergus," said Conrad. "He was a little bigger than Penguin, but he had the same kind of black patches."

I nodded again.

"He died last year. Peacefully, at home, of old age."

"I'm sorry," I said. It sounds weird, but that's what you're supposed to say to a person who's lost someone. You're not apologizing to them; you're telling them you know they're in pain and you wish they weren't.

"Thanks," said Conrad. "I miss him every single day."

Penguin was back to nosing around, looking for other things he could choke on. I'd stopped crying and hyperventilating, but I was still hiccupping and shaking. I knew Conrad probably had to get back to whatever he'd been doing before I almost killed my dog, but I was glad he'd decided to sit with me for a minute.

"Here's my mom," I said as a crazy lady in pajamas and untied sneakers ran toward us.

She grabbed me and hugged me, and she did the same to Penguin. Then she turned to Conrad. "You must be the person who saved him," she said. She tried to smooth her wild hair with one hand and failed. "Pardon my outfit. I'm Kate, and this is Emma, and of course Penguin. We are so, so grateful to you. Please, let us do something to thank you."

"I'm Conrad," he said. They shook hands. "And you're welcome. No thanks necessary."

"Oh, no, please. Let us do something, anything. I do tech support, I could give you some free hours, or we could . . . clean your oven or something . . ."

It was probably dawning on Mom, as it was dawning on me, that Conrad was tall, in great shape, and low-key gorgeous. I could tell she was kicking herself for being unwashed and unbrushed and half-dressed in front of this amazing guy, who was not just a hero but also a legit fox.

Conrad laughed and pulled out a business card from his wallet. It said CONRAD PALAIS, TECHNICAL SUPPORT SPECIALIST.

"Trade you," he said, smiling. He handed her the card.

Mom laughed and patted her pajama pockets. "I seem to have left my wallet upstairs," she said.

"Then put your number in my phone. We have to compare business strategies."

Mom's eyes widened just a smidge, then she got it together. "Of course," she said. She entered her number into his phone and gave it back. "And please, if you think of a way we can try to repay you for your kindness, let me know."

"I will," he said. "The oven thing sounded pretty good, actually."

I was finally composed enough to stand and speak like a human being. "You're like the greatest person I ever met," I said.

He smiled. "It was a pleasure to meet you, Emma. Kate, I hope we'll be in touch soon. And Penguin . . ."

Penguin looked up at his savior and wagged his tail.

"Don't bite off more than you can chew."

He winked and walked away. Mom and I stood there like dummies. Then she turned and hugged me tightly. "I'm so glad you guys are okay."

"Me too."

We started walking home. I checked the time—I would have to hustle, or I'd be super late for school.

Mom sighed. "We are so, so, so lucky that he was there to help you," she said. "So, so, so lucky."

"*So* lucky," I agreed.

I put my hand in my pocket, where I'd stashed the new letter. I would never doubt my luck again. Whoever was behind it, whether it was Fran the Super or Dumbledore or Santa Claus—that didn't matter. All that mattered were those two words:

It's real.

Ten

THAT SATURDAY, MOM CAME TO PICK ME up from an afternoon shift at Waggytail. I loved volunteering there on the weekend. Lots of people came in looking to adopt, and I got to help some of them decide which dog was right for them. It was wonderful (and just a little sad) when we had empty cages at the end of the day.

I saw Mom come through the door, but she didn't see me. Wesley, one of the other volunteers, greeted her and asked her what kind of dog she was looking for.

"One that's about four foot ten," she said, looking around for me. "With dark hair, tan skin, and a phone stuck to her hand."

Wesley stood there for a sec with a question mark floating over his head.

Then Mom spotted me. "Aha! There she is. She's perfect. I'll take her."

I was finished with everything—I just had to grab the handy roll of masking tape and use it to get some of the dog hair off me.

Meanwhile, Mom chatted with Holly. "I might know someone who's ready to adopt," said Mom. "I'll send him here as soon as he makes up his mind."

"Great," said Holly. "If he's a friend of yours, I know he'll provide a good home for one of our pups."

As we walked to the subway, I wanted to ask Mom if the friend she mentioned was Conrad. I hoped so. Conrad was a miraculous dog-saving angel, and the more Mom thought about Conrad, the less she would think about "Dare."

"Dare," as in "I *dare* you to creep on my mom when you already have a girlfriend."

Also as in "The guy we were on our way to meet at Herbie's house so we could look over the archive."

"The archive," as in "all of Herbie's old films and photos."

Also as in "the excuse my mom and Darren kept using so they could FaceTime each other constantly and say it was 'work-related.'"

Work-related, I scoffed to myself. *I bet that's what he tells his girlfriend, Pauline, when he calls Mom.*

Lucky for Mom, I was on the case. Sure, Darren *seemed* like the Southern gentleman he claimed to be. He *appeared* considerate and funny and sweet. He *acted* kind of like a younger, less cranky, straight version of Herbie, who Mom liked so much. But he couldn't fool me. Something about him was shady.

I mean, he looked innocent enough when we got uptown and saw him there, sitting outside on the front stoop, enjoying the evening air. He hopped up and smiled widely as soon as he saw us. "Hey, Kate and Emma, good to see you."

I waved and kept my distance. He and Mom embraced briefly and pecked each other's cheeks. Acquaintance kisses were permissible under Aunt Jenny's rules, but I would have preferred to see a handshake. A handshake was businesslike, and this was business.

We followed Darren inside the house.

"I started looking at some of the film footage," he said excitedly as he led us toward the dining room. "I can't wait to show it to you. I kind of wish I hadn't sold all the furniture, though. I had to improvise a screening room. Right this way . . ."

He presented the room with a flourish. Darren had purchased three beanbag chairs and set his laptop on a small carton. I noticed three individual bowls of popcorn by the chairs—Mom must have told him how much I loathe eating popcorn from the same bowl as other people, with their saliva-covered fingers touching my kernels. The separate bowls were a nice touch, but they were also a bad sign. My enemy was cleverer than I thought.

"Unfortunately," Darren said, "the screen isn't huge, so we'll have to sit kind of close."

HA HA HA! I'm weak. The "we'll have to sit kind of close" thing was such a middle school move. No doubt, Darren wanted to sit close to Mom so he could yawn and stretch and casually put his arm around her.

"Oh, this is great!" Mom said cheerfully. She sat down on the middle beanbag, effectively ruining my plan to sit between them. I took the seat to her right, closer to the door.

Darren leaned over the laptop and opened a file. "It's really incredible footage. We're so lucky Herbie knew someone with a movie camera. This was state-of-the-art technology back then."

The video started. It had no sound, just that *clickety-clickety* noise that very old movies have, and the picture was jumpy, like it was slightly sped up. The two handsome young men from the photo album sprang to life—Herb and Jack, together again, frolicking in the surf on Fire Island. The color of the film was faded like an Instagram filter, but the bright beauty of the day shone through.

Herb and Jack went from splashing each other to tossing around a football to doing a cancan dance with some other young men on the sand. The scenes went quickly and ran right into each other. There were Herbie and Jack in various settings: sitting on the deck of a beachfront home at sunset, toasting with their martini glasses to whoever was behind the camera, hugging in front of the fireplace.

"They loved each other so much," Mom said wistfully. There was a pang of sadness in her voice.

"They were together for forty-five years," Darren said. "They were best friends."

The video clicked and jumped, and suddenly we were here in this house, where a holiday party was under way. The party was lit—you could tell by the way the women reared way back and laughed with their mouths wide open, and by the way the men had untied their ties and unbuttoned their shirts practically to their navels. The guests mugged for the camera as it came by: posing dramatically, performing silly dances, acting out silent melodramas. There was even a guy wearing a lampshade on his head, which he kept lifting so he could sip more of his drink.

Click. We were watching the same party, but now Herb and Jack were standing and making a toast to an elegant dark-haired woman seated nearby. The woman laughed and reached out her foot in its dainty, pointed-toe shoe to kick Jack lightly in the leg. He pretended to crumple from the blow.

"That's Great Aunt Helena," said Darren. "What a great old dame she was. She always used to give us kids the cherries from her drinks. And her drinks were *strong.* Me and my cousins spent every Thanksgiving drunk on cherries. I was heartbroken when she died."

The picture jumped again, this time to a

wedding ceremony in progress. The groom was Herb, the bride was Helena, and the best man was Jack, dressed to the nines in a shiny black tuxedo.

"Herbie married Helena?" I cried, dismayed. (Despite my tough exterior, I can still get deeply emotional about true love.) "How could he do that to Jack?"

"He had to," Mom said. "In those days, your life was in danger if you were openly gay. Lots of gay men had 'arrangements' with female friends so they could stay in the closet. Look, there they all are on the honeymoon cruise."

The picture had jumped to footage of Herbie, Jack, Helena, and her maid of honor, waving from the top deck of a boat. Then they were playing cards, laughing as the wind threatened to whisk their hands away. The women won a game, rejoiced, and exchanged a long kiss. "See?" said Mom. "It worked out okay."

Darren smiled nostalgically. "Uncle Herb wanted all his grandnieces and grandnephews to have what he and Jack had. He told me every time we talked, 'Darren, when you find the right one, don't ever let her go.' "

There was a meaningful silence. I'm pretty sure, if I hadn't been there, violin music would have swelled from nowhere and they would have fallen into each other's arms.

Fortunately, Darren's phone rang.

He looked to see who it was, and his face got stern. Mom paused the video.

"Please excuse me," Darren said, rising quickly and striding toward the hall. "I need to take a quick business call."

Oh ho! Another business call! Darren sure was busy with business.

"I have to whiz," I told Mom. "I'll be right back."

I acted like I was going to the bathroom, then reversed my course. Darren was standing a few feet down the hall, his back turned toward me. I silently crept closer so I could hear what he was saying.

"What do you want?" he said. He didn't sound patient and kind and sweet. He sounded exasperated. "For cryin' out loud, are you serious? The air conditioner is broken? Then call the repair guy!"

My eyes narrowed. This didn't sound like "business." It sounded like a household matter. Whoever was on the phone was chattering so loudly, I thought Darren might be talking to a rabid chipmunk.

"For God's sake, Pauline. What am I supposed to do about it from here?" Pause. "I understand, but you don't have to call me seventeen times! I'm trying to take care of some business here."

Pauline.

"Business."

Exactly as I'd thought.

Now the chipmunk on the phone sounded angry.

Darren was getting angry, too. "I told you, I'll be back on Monday afternoon."

The chipmunk got louder.

"I'm not having this argument with you again. I am here to deal with Uncle Herb's estate. I am meeting with real estate agents all weekend, and I will be back on Monday afternoon. Okay? I'm turning off my phone now. Good night."

He ended the call and groaned quietly to himself. I slithered into another room off the hall just in time for him to turn around. He ran his fingers through his hair, then headed back to where Mom sat innocently, waiting to have her heart stepped on.

I waited another full minute before reentering the living room. When I did, I had a pained look on my face. "Um, Mom?" I mumbled softly, one hand on my lower stomach. "I'm feeling, um, not exactly good."

"Not exactly good" is our code for anything embarrassing, like diarrhea or my period.

Mom nodded at me and rose from her beanbag. "I'm so sorry," she said to Darren. "Unfortunately, we need to go. But I'm loving this footage. Can you put it online somewhere so we can watch the rest of it later?"

"Sure," said Darren. He was trying to cover his disappointment, as was Mom. I could see they didn't want to leave each other. "Or you could come back another time! I'll be back in town soon. Maybe there's a time that's convenient . . ."

I tugged on Mom's shirt a little. Me and my imaginary diarrhea-period needed to get moving before she and Darren could make another date.

"We'll FaceTime this week and set something up," she said as Darren walked us to the door. She gave him a quick acquaintance kiss.

I waved. "Bye, thanks."

Darren closed the door behind us. Mom stopped on the sidewalk and looked at me with concern. "Sorry you're feeling bad, Bloopy. You okay to take the train? Or do we need a taxi?"

I felt guilty about lying to Mom and making her worry when there was nothing really wrong with me. I felt so bad, my stomach actually did start to hurt. I knew a taxi would be expensive, but I couldn't resist.

"Taxi, please," I requested.

Even though her precious, only daughter was unwell, Mom was in a great mood, humming to herself in the cab the whole way downtown. I hadn't seen Mom that happy in months. I wanted to tell her about the phone call I'd overheard, but I didn't want to bring her down. Besides, Mom already knew about Pauline. Mom knew that Darren had a girlfriend, and that didn't stop her from liking him.

If that didn't do it, I didn't know what could.

Eleven

I WAS ONE DAY AWAY FROM THE END OF my lucky month, less than two weeks away from the play, and two minutes away from losing my mind.

I'd given up trying to understand how luck worked. It was like electricity, or the Internet–it didn't matter *how* it worked, as long as it worked. And it was working. It was working so well, it was spooky.

1. Holly offered me an internship for part of the summer. "With the expansion coming up, we need all the help we can get," she explained. The position involved filing and data entry, and Knights Seminary would give me extra credit for it. I couldn't believe I was going to

get more extra credit for hanging out with dogs. It does not get much luckier than that.

2. The dentist canceled my appointment. Has that ever happened in the history of dentistry? Dr. Bander's office was flooded by a neighbor's burst pipe, and she wouldn't be able to see patients for the next two or three months while she had it repaired. Tell me that's just a fluke.
3. Mom made a coffee date with Conrad. And while Mom kept saying that coffee dates are "not romantic, just friendly," I think we both hoped she could be more than friendly with Conrad. Not only would Conrad distract her from Darren, Conrad was handsome and heroic, and if he weren't twenty years older than me, I'd be in love with him, too. Not that Mom was in love with him—yet—but I did catch her stalking him online.

"I'm just looking at his LinkedIn to see if we have any clients in common," she protested.

Oh, Mom, I thought, rolling my eyes. *Please go to Lying School and sign up for the remedial class.*

"He doesn't have Facebook," I informed her. "I already looked."

4. Lewis dropped out of the play.

Ms. Engel broke the news at rehearsal. She'd just spoken to Lewis's dad, who said he was sorry, but urgent family business meant they all had to go to the Philippines the week of the show. Which was *crazy* suspicious, since Lewis Goldstein was not even the slightest bit Filipino.

Ms. Engel was fully furious. She couldn't help yelling at us, even though she knew it wasn't our fault. "How are we supposed to replace our lead actor two weeks before the show? How is someone else going to learn the lines and the blocking in time? We don't even have an understudy!"

"I can do it." Jason, one of the upper school crew members, came forward from backstage. "I've heard it a million times."

Okay, now. This was *way* beyond ordinary luck. This was luck times a million. This was nearing-infinity luck. Jason was a ninth grader, and he was so fully, effortlessly, indescribably hot, it boggled the mind. Looking at him was blinding. Even teachers fell under the spell of his gorgeousness.

"You can't mean it," said Ms. Engel. "You really mean it? Please don't joke around with me right now—I can't take it."

"I'm serious." Jason reached out to shake my hand. "Hey, Emma. I'm Jason."

Hey, Jason, I'm DYING. "Hey," I said.

"If you have an extra copy of the script, I'll use it for today. Then I'm pretty sure I can get the lines down."

Melanie and Ms. Engel looked at each other, openmouthed. "This is incredible," said Ms. Engel. She handed Jason a copy of the script. "This is *literally* incredible."

Her mind was so blown, she used the word "literally," which she hated. We were all banned from using that word in her classroom.

What kind of practical joke was the universe playing on me this time? Suddenly I'd been rescued from the arms of my enemy and placed into the arms of a fourteen-year-old Greek god. Jason stepped into the role of Julian like he'd been there since the beginning. I was the one having trouble with the lines at rehearsal that day—looking at Jason made it hard to speak.

Afterward, I went to the girls' room with Brooke and Geneva so we could scream at each other: "AAAAAAAAAAAAAH!"

Jason replaced Lewis just in time, too. Even after Lewis had helped spread Savvy's picture, I'd been trying to convince myself that maybe he wasn't the most loathsome human being in history. Worse, I kind of didn't mind rehearsing our scenes. Now the thought made me gag. He was a user, a liar, and friends with everyone I hated. He probably wanted to make me think he liked me and then reject me in public, or something awful like that.

But then I'd noticed that he'd done a total turnaround and, tbh, I had no clue why. He no longer looked at me in the hall, in class, outside, or anywhere else. He acted like I didn't exist, and I acted like I didn't care, because I didn't. I did not care at all.

I watched him at lunch that day, sitting at the table of evil. He was tipped back in his chair, laughing at someone else's expense. Dakota cackled loudly. Tyler high-fived him. Venice sat next to Tyler and looked adoring.

"I'm so happy Lewis got out of that stupid play before he turned into a *dramatic actor,*" Dakota said loudly to Sierra.

"They're all such losers," Sierra agreed. "And dirty, scummy rats."

I thought about the "loser" they got to step in for Lewis. If Jason was a loser, I never wanted to win again. According to Melanie's story about karma, I would probably be married to Jason in three years, and Dakota would be in jail for being her heinous self.

I couldn't wait to see how things would work out.

✉

Mom was in the kitchen when I got home, typing like a maniac and cursing ducks. I wanted to ask how her coffee date with Conrad went, but I knew it wasn't the right time.

"Bloop," she said, eyes on her laptop. "You got a letter."

I had several heart attacks in a row. Mom wasn't supposed to know about the letters. How did she know I'd gotten one? Did she read it? If so, would she make me explain the whole thing? And how was I supposed to explain it when I didn't understand it myself? I tried to say something and nearly choked on my own tongue.

Mom was deep into her work, so she was oblivious to my distress. "It's over there on the counter," she said.

Phew. It wasn't a mystery envelope that had been slid under the door. It was just a regular letter, with a stamp and an address and a postmark, delivered by the U.S. Postal Service. I almost forgot those existed. Who even writes letters anymore? I ripped it open to find out.

It was from Savvy.

Dear Emma,

Hey. How are you? I'm not great, but I'm getting better. Every day I wake up and for a second I think it's a normal day, and then I remember what happened, and it makes me want to crawl under my bed and stay there.

Anyway, Moms won't let me have a phone or email or anything, so I'm writing you this letter. Kind of going cray over here with no phone, but it's also good that I don't have contact with anybody from school. I never want to see any of them again.

Moms sent me to a shrink. She's

cool, I guess. She doesn't make me talk about stuff if I don't want to. I don't get the point of it, but I will take any excuse to get out and see people who aren't Moms. I feel so trapped in this house. They got me a home tutor for the rest of the school year, and then they'll decide where I go to high school. I just want to go somewhere where nobody knows me.

How are you? I'm so happy for you that you got the lead in the play. You deserve it. You'll be great! I'm sorry I didn't say congratulations when you got the part, but I didn't know how when we were barely speaking.

I know it's my fault that we weren't speaking, and I'm sorry. I never should have been friends with Dakota and those guys. I miss you a lot. If you want to visit again sometime, that would be great.

You're like the only person Moms would let me see. But I know you're busy with the play and everything else. I wish I could see it.

The note you gave me when you came the other day made me cry so hard. I messed up a lot of things, including our friendship. Being best friends with you is the only thing I miss about my old life.

PLEASE write back even if it's to say you hate me.

Love,
Vannah

PS: I changed my name. I'm not called Savvy anymore. Now I'm Vannah. And I'm dropping A-Mom's last name, so I'll just be Vannah Stone. Remember when we used to play "secret identity"? Now I have one, LOL.

I instinctively reached for my phone to text her before realizing, *Yeah, that's not going to work.* I just wanted to send her some hearts. I didn't have any words yet—I couldn't choose between, *Yeah, you were pretty awful* and *It's okay, I forgive you* since both were true. A heart would have said it all.

Mom finished typing and slammed the laptop lid. "Argh! Duck-knocking hockey puck! Hockey hockey hockey puck puck puck! I told her eight hundred times to back up her data, and now she lost everything and she's blaming me."

Mom's face was bright pink, and she looked to be on the verge of tears. Sometimes she got angry at clients, but this was extreme. I decided to walk Penguin and give her some room to cool down.

Fifteen minutes later, when Penguin and I came back, Mom had returned to speaking English and was typing at only 80 words per minute, instead of 180 per second. "Sorry I was crabby, Bloop. Thanks for walking the dog."

"Sure," I said. Then I ventured, "So how was the coffee date?"

She stopped typing, closed the lid of her laptop, and rolled her eyes. "Oh, it was great!" she said in her most sarcastic voice. "We went to this cute place on University, and we got a nice pot of coffee, and then thirty-seven different women stopped by our table to say hi to Conrad and ask why he hadn't called them."

"What?"

"Yep! He's a total player. One of those guys who needs to have women falling all over him. And he wasn't even embarrassed about it. You remember that first day at Herbie's, when Darren was embarrassed about Pauline calling, and he said it was 'work'? This guy didn't even bother to pretend these women were clients. Ugh!"

Yeah, that's a major ugh. I felt bad for Mom. She was wearing the new shirt she'd bought online *and* paid express shipping for so she'd have it in time to wear today.

"At least he saved Penguin," I said.

"And that's the only reason I didn't flip the table and walk out." Mom sighed. "I should have known Conrad was too good to be true. Oh well. Better luck next time, right?"

Speaking of luck, I still needed to track down Fran and grill her about the letters. "Have you seen Fran?"

"Yeah, she was downstairs when I came in from my amazing dream date. She was about to do the recycling, so she might still be in the basement."

"Oh, great. I need to . . . uh . . ." What did I need to do that involved going to the basement? *Aha!* "I need to see if there are any empty shoe boxes down there. I think I'm going to do a diorama for my, uh, history project."

"What project?" Mom asked, but I was already out the door and down the stairs to the basement.

I heard Fran humming and talking to herself as she mopped the laundry room. I crept toward her, trying to think of what I could say to open the conversation. *Hey, Fran, I got your letter.* Or, *Hey, Fran, thanks for the letter.* Or, *Hey, Fran, WTH is up with the freaky, possibly magical letters you've been sliding under my door?*

I got the first part out: "Hey, Fran."

She jumped about six feet in the air and dropped the mop handle. "Jesus . . . Christ!" she yelled, with a truly impressive assortment of profanities between the "Jesus" and the "Christ." She put one hand over her heart and wheezed. "Tryin' to kill me."

"Sorry," I said. "I didn't mean to sneak up on you."

She looked at me suspiciously as she picked up her mop. "Well, you accidentally did a real good job of it there."

"Sorry. I just had a question—"

"I don't have time for questions right now. And don't step on the clean floor! Just go back up those stairs and let my floor dry before you mess it all up again." Fran turned her back to me and resumed mopping.

"Okay," I said. "But I got this letter—"

"Good for you!" she cried nervously. "Now take your dirty shoeprints upstairs. I don't know anything about your letters."

Fran was definitely hiding something. She kept mopping the same part of the floor so she wouldn't have to turn around and face me. And she said she didn't know about my *letters*. Plural. But I'd only mentioned one letter.

"How did you know there was more than one?"

She threw down the mop in frustration. "I meant all your letters! None of your letters! I don't concern myself with anybody's mail!"

Now, this was just untrue. Fran was a snoop, a gossip, and a meddler, and everyone in the building knew it. Last fall, when Emily Chang got a fat letter from Yale University, the whole building knew she'd been accepted before she even got home from her cello lesson.

Of course Fran had something to do with the letters. Nothing happened in our building without Fran's permission. Last time we talked, she threw me off the trail by playing dumb, but I was onto her now. "Please, Fran, the month's almost over, and I'm dying to know—"

"Bloop?" I heard Mom call from the top of the basement stairs. "I found a shoe box!"

Fran was instantly relieved. "Hey, Kate!" she called. "Tell yer daughter to get her mangy feet off my clean floor!"

Mom's laugh echoed in the stairwell. "Come on up, Bloop! I got what you were looking for."

I looked pleadingly at Fran. She had turned her back to me again. "Fine," I said, then stomped back up the stairs. I'd find another opportunity to confront her. We lived in the same building, so she couldn't avoid me forever. And I was going to get to the bottom of the mystery, one way or another.

One more day.

✉

I sat on my bed that night, thinking about my luck. So much had happened in the last four weeks, I felt like I had aged a year. I barely remembered what my life was like before I got the first letter. It was less complicated back then, for sure. But definitely less interesting than it was now.

I pulled out the first letter and reread it. I had to admit, it didn't sound at all like Fran. I looked over the instructions again.

> This is not a hoax. This is real, and here's how you can prove it:
>
> Write a list of ten lucky little things you want to happen. At the end of the thirty days, look at the list and see what your good luck has brought you.

It wasn't quite the end of the thirty days, but it was close enough. Time to look at the list again, and see what my good luck had brought me.

1. Mom gets me a new phone.

Check. And she gave it to me when I least expected it. And not only was it a new phone, it was a *new* new phone—not one of Mom's old ones, but a nice fresh one straight out of the box. I suddenly realized that Mom could have kept the new phone for herself and given me the phone she was using. I would have been one thousand percent psyched and happy about it. Instead, she gave me the brand-new one and kept using her old phone. That was extremely cool of her, and I hadn't even noticed.

My new phone looked even luckier to me now.

2. Get a speaking part in the spring play.

Check plus. A bad day led to a good audition, which led to me getting the lead. Which led me to star in a love scene with the hands-down-handsomest guy at school. Which was a scene I was going to perform in front of everybody in the auditorium, twice. I was going to get to kiss Jason onstage, right in front of Dakota and her girls, all because they made me cry on audition day. Sweet, sweet karma.

> ~~3. Dakota likes me and invites me to hang out at her house with everyone.~~

X. This one didn't come true, and thank God for that. Fortunately, I crossed it off before it could happen, and replaced it with:

> 3. Dakota leaves me alone.

Okay, still *X*. But if I could find out who told on Tyler, I might get this one to happen, too.

> ~~4. Make out with Tyler Hoff~~
> 4. Make out with a guy I like.

Check, almost? Kissing Jason had to count for at least partial credit, although, strangely, I wasn't as into kissing Jason as I thought I'd be. He had mushy lips that lay there like slugs on mine, and his breath smelled like hot milk. But when I became his girlfriend, I'd fix all that. In the meantime, I'd offer him a mint.

5. Make new friends.

Serious check. Besides Brooke, Harrison, and Geneva, there was Melanie, who was older and cooler than me, *and* was smart and caring and gave good advice. I was starting to annoy Mom because I was on my phone all the time. Perfect.

6. Mom gets a boyfriend or a social life.

X. I thought she'd get to choose between two guys, but neither one was available, and that had just made her feel more alone. Boo.

7. Go somewhere good this summer instead of Grandma's.

Check-ish. I wasn't going someplace exotic and amazing, but I had my summer internship at Waggytail, so I wouldn't be stuck in the city with nothing to do. And Holly let me know that I could take a week off each month to go to the beach with Mom and Penguin. Grandma's wasn't looking so bad after all, since I wouldn't be there all summer. Maybe I'd even bring Brooke or Geneva with me for a few days. And I'd be able to tell Bobby Dudderman what happened with the letter. If he even cared.

While Bobby was on my mind, I searched for him on Instagram and was mildly surprised to find him there. Most of his posts were of rocks and shells and feathers. There was only one self-portrait of him, standing on the beach in a tank top. He'd obviously been hitting the gym and putting some thought into his appearance. The short haircut looked good on him, and, if my eyes did not deceive me, he was wearing Billabong shorts.

Good for you, Bobby the Dud, I thought. *May the odds be ever in your favor.*

Surprisingly, Bobby had a ton of followers, and many of his posts got lots of comments. A lot of his followers were adults, some from other countries, and there were even some girls who followed him. I frowned at the pic next to lacysnowflake's comment. She was pretty cute. She must have thought he was pretty cute, too, judging by her comments. I mean, it's just a seashell—it doesn't deserve *that* many exclamation points.

Anyway.

~~**8.** Mom forgets my upcoming dentist appointment.~~

Check-ish. She didn't forget, but I didn't have to go to the dentist anyway. And that was even after I crossed this one out and replaced it with:

8. Help Savvy.

X. Once Tyler got that picture, there was no way I could have helped Savvy. She couldn't avoid the consequences of her decision, and now she was disgraced and embarrassed and stuck at home with two angry moms. It was severe punishment for a single mistake. At the start of the month, I was so mad at her that I would have been happy to hear she was grounded for life. Now I felt heartsick for her. As Melanie had discovered with her anorexic friend, karma could be sweet, but it could also be bitter.

9. Savvy stops being weird to me.

Well, check. But I didn't want it to happen like this. If I could choose between Savvy being snotty, or Vannah's life being ruined, I would take Snotty Savvy any day. But it wasn't my wish that caused this whole chain of events to start—was it?

I went back to the original letter. It didn't say anything about "granting wishes" or "making things come true." It just told me to watch what happened.

> You will not know when these lucky things are coming. You may not recognize some of them when you see them. Some, like this money, will be obvious right away. Others will take time to reveal themselves.

So if I didn't know the lucky thing was coming, and I wouldn't even recognize it when I saw it, how could I be the source of it? I couldn't. What had happened to Savvy was not my doing. My good luck didn't cause her downfall; her bad luck did.

Well, if nothing else happened on my last lucky day, I would at least get some kind of explanation. Or so I hoped. I hoped so hard that there would be a letter on the floor the next morning while Mom slept in, one that would explain the whole crazy month—all the coincidences, all the lucky breaks, how it all worked, and who was behind it.

But what if there was no letter? What if the last day passed, and that was it? What if I never ever heard anything from the letter writer ever again? That would be too cruel. The curiosity would kill me. I wouldn't be able to deal with never knowing the truth. *Please,* I thought. *Don't keep me in the dark. Send me another letter, like you did last time I had doubts. But this time, say more than "It's real." Tell me how it works.*

At least there was one thing I could count on: One more day, and I could tell Mom about everything. Once the month was over, the *No human person must know* rule wouldn't matter anymore. It's not like whoever it was could take the luck back. They couldn't rewind to the beginning of the month. It would be such a relief to talk about it, finally, to show Mom the letter and see what she thought. One more day.

I put the list and letter away. It would all be over soon. My special good luck would be gone. The universe had just twenty-four hours to send me the name of Tyler's rat, a boyfriend for Mom, and a way to help Savvy. Not to mention the impossible, the last lucky little thing on my list:

10. Bring Aunt Jenny back.

Twelve

MY LAST LUCKY DAY STARTED MUCH like my first one did: with dog snot.

I was wide awake in an instant. It felt like Christmas morning—I couldn't wait to run into the kitchen to see if Santa had brought me the gift of an explanation. But if there was a letter for me, Mom had already seen it, since she was already up. I could hear her shuffling around, talking to someone on her earpiece.

I went to the bathroom, rinsed my face, and headed toward the kitchen. Letter or no letter, I was excited to see what this day would bring.

I overheard Mom say, "I know, Florence. I know."

I stopped dead in my tracks. Florence was Aunt Jenny's mom. Today was Aunt Jenny's birthday.

And I forgot.

How could I forget? I was disgusted with myself. Here I was, supposedly so sad over Aunt Jenny's death, and I forgot her birthday. I still missed her all the time, but I'd been so distracted these past few weeks, busy obsessing over friends and phones and luck and dentist appointments, she had somehow slipped my mind.

So much for *Bring Aunt Jenny back*.

Last year for Aunt Jenny's birthday, the three of us went to the crafts store and got a bunch of stuff and decorated her apartment for the birthday party she was having that night. We made tissue-paper flowers and strung them into garlands; then we tied different-colored ribbons around all the lamps and clocks and knickknacks so that everything in the house looked like a present. Everybody loved it when they came in and saw what we'd done.

I gave Aunt Jenny a pin shaped like a horseshoe crab. I'd had to order it online, and it took a month to ship from China. I was so afraid it wouldn't get here in time, and I cried with frustration every morning it didn't arrive, but then it showed up the day before the party. I'd wrapped it in paper that had lobsters on it (that was the closest I could find to crab wrapping paper), and when she opened the box and saw it, she burst out laughing with tears in her eyes.

"This is the most perfect gift ever!" She gave me a huge hug and kissed the top of my head. "And you are the most perfect girl."

We had no idea it would be her last birthday.

I stood in the hall and listened as Mom wrapped up her call. "I know . . . She was . . . Always . . . Okay, I'll tell her . . . Be well . . . Bye."

She ended her call and let out a super-long "Phhhewwwwww."

I went into the kitchen and hugged her.

"Bloop," she said.

I didn't say anything, just kept hugging her. I didn't hug Mom a lot anymore, not since my boobs had started their slow, awkward expansion into the world. But I didn't care right then. She needed a hug.

I could feel her rib cage shake as she began crying. I was way ahead of her there. Her tears fell on my head, and mine soaked into her pajama top.

"I miss her so much," said Mom.

"Me too."

Mom reached for the paper towels on the counter, blew her nose in one, and offered me another. I detached myself and mopped up my face. So far that morning, my face had been covered in both dog snot and human snot, and it was only seven-fifteen.

Mom started making her coffee and I poured myself some juice.

"Florence says hello," she said.

Hi, Florence, I said in my head. Funny, how I saw Florence at the hospital nearly every day for weeks, and now weeks went by without me even thinking about her.

Mom continued. "She's finally sending Jenny's ashes, so we can take them out to the beach and release them over the bay."

I nodded, not trusting myself to speak without starting to cry all over again.

If only there was a letter for me in the kitchen, the letter I'd been hoping for, the one that would explain my lucky month. But there was no letter on the floor by the door, and there was no letter on the counter, the table, or anywhere else I could see.

I showered, dressed, and walked the dog while Mom muttered at her laptop. I returned Penguin and was ready to leave for school when I casually asked, "Oh, uh, I didn't get a letter, did I?"

Mom was busy responding to an email from yet another duck-knocking hockey puck. "When? Yesterday? Not that I saw. Today's mail won't be here until this afternoon. Why?"

"Nothing important. I thought I might have got another letter from Savv—Vannah."

I headed out to school. I felt extremely blah and gray about everything. There had been no letter, which meant there would probably be no letter, and I would never understand what had been happening to me. On top of that, I was really mad at myself for being such a shallow, disloyal person that I forgot Aunt Jenny's birthday. I'd promised I would never forget her, I would think about her every day, and I would keep her alive in my heart. But I was already letting her memory slip away, already back to concentrating on my life instead of her loss.

✉

I sleepwalked through the day. Nothing mattered. Our lives were short and dumb and meaningless. And random—life was also really, really random. It could end at any time, for any reason, just like it did for Aunt Jenny. Maybe I'd start dressing like Melanie and go the tortured-artist route.

I was about to go into rehearsal after school when someone's arm shot out from the shadows by the trophy case and grabbed me. I was shocked to discover that it was Lewis.

"What do you want?" I hissed at him, pulling away. "Get off me."

He pulled me back. "Emma, it's an emergency. Tyler and Dakota are at it again, and if you don't help me stop them, Venice is going to get hurt." His voice was low and urgent, and his eyes were the eyes I remembered from our time onstage. Suddenly he'd switched back from Lewis the Troll to Just Plain Lewis. I liked Just Plain Lewis, but I couldn't trust him.

"Is this a joke?" I asked. "Are you getting back at me for ratting on Tyler? Because I didn't."

"I know you didn't," he said. "And this is not a joke. I wish it was. They've been working on Venice for two weeks. They want her to pose for a pic for Tyler, just like Savvy did. They're gonna make her do it at Dakota's this afternoon—unless we can stop them."

Whoa. What? He was going too fast for me. Lewis was friends with those people, so why was he telling me this stuff? What was I supposed to do about it? "They're your friends," I said. "You stop them."

"They *were* my friends," he said. "And I'm not even sure that's true. Listen, I know you can't trust me, but you *can* trust Dakota and Tyler to be themselves. You know the kind of things they do. You saw what they did to Savvy. Don't let it happen to someone else."

I had to decide quickly. On the one hand, I had Lewis the Troll feeding me this "emergency" news designed to make me act stupid in front of everyone. On the other hand, here was Lewis, my friend from the play, asking me to help him stop Venice from getting hurt.

I thought about Savvy, shut up at home like

Rapunzel, and how ashamed she felt. I thought about Venice, how eager to please she was, and how she could get caught in the same trap.

If I was being set up to look stupid, then I'd look stupid.

"What do you need me to do?"

Lewis let out a huge sigh of relief. "Okay. They're all heading over to Dakota's soon. I'll stall Tyler as long as possible. You get outside, find Venice, and tell her she's being set up. She's not going to believe you. You'll have to convince her any way you can. Text me if you need help."

"Got it."

Lewis and I shared a look. It was like that day onstage, when I could read his mind through his eyes. *Thank you for believing me,* his look said. Then he darted away.

Just then, Ms. Engel came around the corner and caught a glimpse of Lewis running down the hall. "Ah," she said to me. "Our runaway Julian."

The words rushed out of my mouth. "Ms. Engel, I'm sorry, I can't come to rehearsal today."

Ms. Engel did a double take. "Are you kidding me? You're kidding me. This is a joke."

"I'm sorry," I said. "It's urgent."

She looked at me like I wasn't speaking English. Then she laughed in my face. "Hah!" she said. "It's urgent? Are you going to the Philippines with your friend Lewis?"

"It's not like that, please, I can explain–"

Ms. Engel cut me off. "You know, we found a replacement for him. I could just as easily get one of the other girls in the cast to replace you."

I didn't want that to happen. But I didn't want anything to happen to Venice either. "I'm sorry," I said, backing away down the hall. "I promise, I'll explain."

I thought Ms. Engel was going to have a stroke, she was so mad. "Hey, Emma!" she called after me. "*Good luck* with your urgent thing!"

Ms. Engel's curse would not stop me. I ran

outside the building and looked around, but I didn't see Venice. Lewis was hanging out with Tyler and Dakota's group, and I paused for a minute. He saw me and motioned with his head toward the corner. There was Venice, coming back from the store with some Swedish fish.

I ran up to intercept her. "Venice, listen. Really important. Tyler and Dakota are trying to get you to send him nudes."

Venice drew back in surprise and wrinkled her nose. "What are you talking about?"

Dakota was already looking our way, scowling at the sight of me talking to Venice.

"You know what they did to Savvy? They got her picture and they spread it. They're trying to do the same thing to you."

Venice rolled her eyes and pushed past me. "You're pathetic. I'm sorry I was ever nice to you."

"Please!" I urged. "Just don't go over to Dakota's house today!"

But she was already walking away.

Lewis saw her coming and looked alarmed. "Guys, wait. Before we go to Dakota's, we need to, uh, get snacks! Yeah, I'm not trying to mess with those soggy-ass chips her mom buys. Ty, come hit the deli with me."

Tyler shrugged at Dakota. "We'll meet you over there in a minute," he said. He followed Lewis toward the store.

Venice was surrounded by the girls. I couldn't get anywhere near her. She'd given me her phone number the day the cast list went up, so I could at least text her, but how was I going to convince her to stay away from Tyler by text? What could I possibly text her that would make her believe he was lying scum?

I didn't know. But I bet Savvy did.

I took off running down the block. It was only a short run to Savvy's place, so I could make it in five minutes if I pushed myself. I ran as fast as I could, and when I got to her building, I slammed the buzzer, barely able to breathe.

Charise answered. "Who . . . ?"

"Emma," I gasped. "Emergency!"

She buzzed me in right away, and I flew up the stairs. Ava was home early from court, so both moms were standing in the hall looking alarmed.

"Emma," said Charise. "What happened? Are you hurt?"

I shook my head. "Not me. But someone. Please, I need Savvy's help."

Charise and Ava looked at me skeptically. "All right," Charise said. "But this better be good." She let me into the apartment, where I ran to Savvy's side.

"What's happening?" Savvy asked. "Are you okay?"

I shook my head no. "Tyler and Dakota . . . doing it to Venice . . . Have to stop her."

Charise's and Ava's faces hardened at the sound of those names. Savvy flinched, but she could see by the look on my face how urgent this was.

"What can I do?" she asked.

I was already texting faster than I'd ever texted before.

Tyler is fake & I can prove

Seconds later, Venice texted back: one single, smiling poop.

Of course. Why would she believe a loser like me? Especially since she knew I hated Tyler and Dakota. I needed some good, solid evidence. And that's what I came here for.

My fingers were poised over my phone. "Okay, now tell me *exactly* what Tyler said to you when he was trying to hook up with you."

Savvy looked embarrassed. "He said I was ethereal."

I texted Venice:

He said ur ethereal

"Good. What else?"

"He said I made the other girls look superficial, and he was tired of superficial girls."

Ava rolled her eyes. I texted quickly.

Hes tired of superficial girls

Still no reply from Venice.

"Hurry!" I said. "Something else!"

"Um, his dad told him he needed a girl with courage and passion."

His dad said girls shd have courage and passion

Nothing. I prayed that Venice would reply. I was a thousand percent sure that Tyler used the exact same lines on every girl, but what if I was wrong?

We held our breaths and waited. The reply bubble popped up. She was replying!

Ur jells cuz he ddnt like you

"It's not working!" I cried. "Gimme more!"

Savvy desperately tried to come up with something. "That's all I can remember!"

Ava and Charise shared a look. Charise nodded, and Ava ran into the bedroom. When she came back, she was holding Savvy's confiscated phone.

"Here," she said, turning it on. "Screenshot his texts and send them. You only have three percent battery, so hurry."

Savvy's fingers couldn't move fast enough. She took a screenshot and sent it to Venice's number.

I was thinking about you last night. You owe me new sheets. ;)

Then another one:

Dakota's jealous of you. She's never seen me get like this over a girl.

And a third:

> Don't be immature. Send the pic or you're a tease.

We stared at the phone, hoping for a miracle. Venice replied a minute later:

> LOL.

The four of us looked at one another helplessly. "What do we do now?" asked Ava.

Just then, I got a text from Lewis. It was a picture of the cool-kids table taken that afternoon, with Tyler standing in the lunchroom and Venice sitting nearby. Venice did not see the face that Tyler was making behind her back, nor did she see his gesture. She didn't see that Dakota and Sierra were there, laughing and pointing at her.

We all winced. I didn't want to hurt Venice's

feelings, but she needed to see this. I texted it to her.

We didn't have to wait long for her reply:

☹
☹☹
☹☹☹

Ouch. That picture must have been painful for her to see. I was glad she knew the truth, but I wasn't glad that she was hurt by it. I texted:

I'm sorry.

Venice:

No its good thanks Emma
Going home now cu tmrw

"Oh, thank God," said Ava. She hugged Charise, then they both hugged Savvy. It looked like they were coming after me next, but I sidestepped them. I had to text Lewis and let him know that Venice was safe.

It worked! She left! You saved her!

He replied:

YES!

And then a bunch of dancing girls.

I wanted to hang out for a minute more with Savvy and her moms, have some of Charise's homemade mint lemonade and catch my breath, but I'd already missed forty-five minutes of rehearsal. If I left right away, I could run back in time to apologize to Ms. Engel and explain. I grabbed my stuff and prepared to leave.

"Thank you for letting me in," I said to Charise.

"I'm glad you came to us," she said. "You did the right thing."

Savvy and I hugged. "Thanks," she said. "I'll write to you soon."

As I ran back to school, I planned what to say to Ms. Engel. I wanted to tell her the whole story, how Lewis warned me that Venice was in danger, and how we acted together to rescue her. I flew through the school door and burst into the auditorium. Everyone turned to see who it was. Jason was onstage, rehearsing our love scene with Melanie.

Ms. Engel saw me and gave me a vicious smile. "Emma, how sweet of you to join us. I was just telling the cast that I needed to thank you. If you hadn't skipped out on rehearsal today, we wouldn't have known what a terrific actress Melanie is."

"I'm sorry," I said. "Please, let me explain . . ."

"No need," she said. "You're no longer in the show. Melanie is now playing the part of Nadine. Thanks so much, and goodbye."

Ms. Engel turned her back on me. Melanie

looked at me from the stage and frowned. *What happened?* she mouthed.

I'll text you, I pantomimed.

"Goodbye, Emma," said Ms. Engel.

I turned around, hung my head, and left the auditorium.

✉

The second Mom heard my key in the door, she started applauding. "Hooray for Bloop!" she crowed when I walked in. "I heard from Savvy's moms! You're a legit hero!"

Ava and Charise must have called Mom the second I left and filled her in on what happened. She hugged me for way too long, raving the entire time.

"I am so proud of you! That was such quick thinking, to go to Savvy's. That Venice girl is incredibly lucky that you got her away from those kids before anything could happen. You are so smart, and brave, and selfless, and you did great work today, just great."

"Thanks." It didn't feel so great, now that it cost me my leading role. But it could have been worse. I imagined showing up to school in the morning and seeing everyone buzzing over a picture of Venice. At least that wouldn't happen now.

Mom broke out of the hug, drew her head back, and looked at my expression. "What's wrong?" she asked, concerned. "The girl's okay now, right?"

I dropped into a chair and put my head down on the table. *Might as well give her the news,* I thought.

"Ms. Engel cut me from the show because I skipped rehearsal."

I couldn't see her face, but I heard the shock in her voice. "Oh, Bloopster! That's awful! I'm so sorry. But won't she reconsider once you tell her what happened?"

I didn't dare hope for that. "I want to tell her the whole thing, but I don't want to get anybody in trouble. And she was extra mad at me when I said I needed to miss rehearsal. I don't even know if she'll listen to me."

"Oh, wow. That's so unfair. You went out of your way to help someone! You did the right thing! You shouldn't be penalized for it."

"Yeah," I said miserably. Then I said something I never thought I'd say, something Mom used to say when I was younger that drove me crazy. "Life's not fair."

Life was totally unfair. Aunt Jenny was fine in September; in October, she was diagnosed with a terminal disease. Savvy thought she was falling in love; instead, she was falling into a trap. Mom lost her best friend, and she couldn't even have one nice date with a guy to help her feel less lonely. Somebody promised me good luck, but they never told me why.

It was only five o'clock, but it felt like midnight. I couldn't imagine trying to explain to Melanie and Brooke and the rest of my friends why I missed rehearsal—all that typing seemed impossible with my thick, heavy hands. Why bother.

"Bloop," said Mom sympathetically. "You've had such a stressful day. Why don't you lie down on the couch and watch cartoons for a while? I can take Penguin out. We'll have whatever you want for dinner, even if it's cupcakes with ice cream. You deserve a treat."

If only everybody got what they deserved. I slunk over to the couch and got under the quilt and turned on the TV. Mom dimmed the lights and put on Penguin's leash and they went out for a walk.

By the time they got back, I was asleep.

Lucky Thirteen

SOMETIMES YOU NEVER FIND OUT WHY things happened the way they did.

There was no third letter the next morning. There was only a sneezing dog and a gray sky. Mom was still asleep, which was understandable—she wasn't the one who crashed out in front of the TV before six last night, awakened just long enough to stumble into bed, and then slept until the alarm rang. More than twelve hours of sleep, and I was still exhausted.

I went through my morning routine, then took Penguin for his walk. Just like any other ordinary day.

We passed the bench where we'd met Conrad. I thought back to that day, how I'd been scouring the second letter for clues and didn't notice that Penguin had eaten a chicken bone. What kind of lucky letter distracts you so your dog can choke half to death? That wasn't lucky at all. Then Conrad came along, which seemed like the best possible luck, but we wouldn't have needed Conrad's help if I hadn't been busy with the letter, and then Mom wouldn't have been disappointed when he turned out to be a womanizer.

Mom was awake when Penguin and I got back. "Bloop," she said. "How are you feeling today?"

Good question. I had no idea how I felt, because I didn't feel much of anything. "Okay," I lied.

She knew I was lying, but she let it go. "Well, I'm meeting Darren up at Herbie's today to give him the archives on hard disk, and then we're done. Shouldn't take too long. I'll be back by the time you get home from rehears . . . school."

Ugh. Rehears-school. It was time for me to go to school and face the music (or, in this case, the drama). I said bye to Mom and trudged toward my destiny.

I lingered around the corner from school, waiting until it was exactly time to go in. I didn't want to face my theater friends yet. I didn't want to face anybody. The idea of walking into Ms. Engel's English class made me nauseated.

"Hey," said Lewis, coming up behind me. "I was looking for you."

"Hey," I said.

I didn't know what else to say. We'd just gone through this big ordeal together, but mostly it was by text, and now we were face-to-face. It looked like he didn't know what to say, either. I looked at my shoes.

"So," he said. "You want to go to the play with me?"

I had to laugh. Then I sighed. "I don't think Ms. Engel wants to see either one of us ever again.

Besides, aren't you supposed to be in the Philippines?"

"Coincidentally, my family's plans have changed."

We were going to be late if we didn't hurry down the block and through the doors. In a few minutes, the school security guards would sweep the vicinity, looking for stragglers like us. But I didn't know when we'd get another chance to talk in person and in private, and I was curious about a few things.

"So why did you back out of the play?" I asked. "That was kind of a dick move."

"I know," he said. "I wish I hadn't. But it was hard being your stage boyfriend without feeling . . . things. Ty and them were already on me to quit—I didn't want to, but then after the Savvy thing, you hated my guts so much . . . It was way too confusing. Seemed easier to just walk away."

Yeah, I did kind of hate him a lot back then.

I still wasn't exactly sure how I felt about him now, but it wasn't hatred. It might have even been . . . things.

"I get why you hated me, by the way," he continued. "What they did to Savvy was awful, and I didn't stop them. I thought it was a joke. I don't think I understood how serious it was until I saw your face that morning, then I was like, 'Oh, this is the worst possible thing you could do to someone.' I was already starting to look at those guys and wonder why I was friends with them. But that's when I made up my mind. So I told Mr. Kelly."

Splat. Pieces of my exploded brain hit the inside of my skull. "*You* told on Tyler?"

Lewis smiled wryly and nodded. "I did. I'm the rat. And I knew that if those guys found out it was me, it'd be *bad*. You hated me anyway, so I quit the play, and I've been acting like everything's the same as always with Dakota and them, like we're all friends and I think it's hilarious to get girls to send nudes to Tyler. Then I heard they were planning to do it to Venice. And I couldn't sit there and let that happen again." He picked up my hand and caressed it with his thumb, the way he'd done that day onstage. "But I couldn't have stopped them without you."

My hand throbbed in his. If he didn't let it go, it was going to burst into a profound sweat, along with the rest of my body. "We should go in," I said nervously. "We're going to get marked late."

"Then one more second won't matter," he said.

He pulled me toward him and kissed me.

I died.

I recovered.

I kissed him back.

I died again.

Then I heard the sounds of a walkie-talkie coming toward us—school security was on its way. We broke apart and started running toward the school.

"Text me," he huffed, booking it up the stairs and through the doors.

"Yep," I confirmed.

✉

I wish I could say that the rest of the day went smoothly, but it didn't. I tried to talk to Ms. Engel before English, but she refused to hear me out.

"If what you have to say is important, you can put it in writing," she said.

"I'll try," I said glumly, knowing it was hopeless. Where to begin? There was no way I could name names on paper and hand it to a teacher. I slunk back to my desk, where I was ignored for the rest of the period.

At lunch, my first priority was Melanie. She was out eating lunch with her upper school friends, so I sat down alone in the library to compose several lengthy texts that I hoped would explain the situation. I sent parts one and two, which covered the urgent request for help from the shadows and the mission I was charged with, and I was working on part three when Melanie appeared next to me.

"Quick," she urged me. "Come to the third-floor girls' room and tell me everything. *This* is drama."

At least Melanie understood.

"Maybe we can convince Ms. Engel to listen to you," she said after I wrapped up my tale and she swore to keep it quiet. "I'm really not meant to be an actress. And Jason is nice, but he can't kiss *at all.*"

I was not optimistic. "Even if she listens, she already made the decision to cut me. She's not going to go back on it now."

"We'll see," Melanie said, arching one eyebrow. "I've been told I have a way with words."

I didn't see Venice until sixth-period social studies. She gave me a small wave and a sad smile. I returned both.

Sierra noticed our exchange and frowned at Venice. "Don't talk to her," Sierra said. "You'll get her rat fleas."

So it went, on that not-magical, not-lucky day—which, when I thought about it, felt a lot like the lucky days I'd just lived through. Good things and bad things happened, like always:

I'd had my first real, offstage kiss with a boy I liked!

But Ms. Engel was still keeping me out of the show.

Melanie wanted to fight for me!

But Dakota and Sierra wanted to fight me.

My day went up and down, like everyone else's. My lucky days, I realized, had been the same. Before the letters and during the letters and after the letters, my luck wasn't any different. It was bad and then good and then bad and then good again. Strange things happened, and I didn't know why. As Bobby Dudderman said, that was the definition of life.

Suddenly, I got it. My luck had not really changed.

I had.

✉

I was getting ready for my last class, gym, when somebody started blowing up my phone. To my surprise, that person was Mom.

It didn't look like Mom at first. Mom is meticulous about her spelling and punctuation in texts, and these texts were a mess. She must have sent them in a rush. They read:

Pauline si his ex

separate 3 yrs

they run busines together

but hes selling andmoving to harlem

There was a pause, then another text:

HIS EX

I gasped. Pauline was Darren's *ex*? Could that really be true? I replied right away:

NO WAY

Mom:

YESWAY
it rly ws busines after al
omw home
will tell u evrything latr
sooooooooooooo happy

Then there was an emoji avalanche like I'd never seen.

I blinked and reread the texts, finding it hard to believe my eyes. My mind was *beyond blown.* This was the best news in the *history of news.* Darren was *not* a creeper, he *didn't* have a girlfriend, and *it rly ws busines after al.* I nearly burst into happy tears, but I didn't.

I DIDN'T.

It was those allergies again.

✉

After the last bell rang and I realized I had nowhere to be, the allergies started to come back—the sad ones, this time. I felt like a ghost, floating around all the other groups on the sidewalk, unseen by people as I passed. I wanted to share my good news—I kissed Lewis! And Mom might have a boyfriend!—but all my friends were at rehearsal and there was nobody around I could tell. Just like the day I'd gotten the first letter.

I headed home. At least I could share the good part of my day with Mom, and she could share hers with me. I knew she'd be pacing around the kitchen, giddy with excitement, wishing she could call her best friend, as I wished I could call mine.

Mom and I were lucky to have each other.

It was drizzling a little by the time I rounded the corner to my block. To my surprise, there was Fran, hanging out in front of the building, smoking a Lucky in the rain. My heart started to beat fast, and I picked up my pace, ready to run and tackle her to the ground, if need be, so I could get some answers from her. But before I could open my mouth to say anything, she said, "All right, kid. Come get your letter."

Fran stubbed out her smoke, opened the front door, and motioned for me to go inside.

"It *was* you," I marveled, following her to her apartment behind the stairs.

Fran unlocked her door, plucked an envelope from inside, and handed it to me. "See for yourself," she said.

It was a white envelope the same size as the other two, but when I opened it, I found a handwritten letter instead of a printed one. The handwriting was familiar, but shaky and faint. I looked down at the signature.

It was from Aunt Jenny.

Dear Emma,

I miss you.

It seems strange to say this, since you're ten feet away in the waiting room as I write this letter, and I will be gone by the time you read it. But at the moment I miss you so much I can't stand it.

I know after I'm gone, you'll be missing me, too. That's why I'm writing this now.

As you know, the doctors say I don't have a lot of time left, and these pain meds they're giving me are strong. So I'm asking the nurses to mail a package for me today. It's addressed to your super, Fran, and it will contain three letters and some instructions. The first instruction is to keep this all a secret. (If Fran doesn't, I will haunt her *so hard*.)

Fran will give you the first letter six weeks after I go. I have a feeling you'll be running low on hope around then, so this letter will tell you how lucky you are, and how lucky you will be. You'll see: When you think of yourself as lucky, you notice all the good things in your life. You see all the connections between what you do and what happens next. You watch the amazing, mysterious, coincidental ways the world works, and you will be awestruck.

The letter will tell you to write down ten things you want to happen, because that's the first step to getting what you want in life: deciding what that is. Some of those things will happen for you, some won't, and some will turn into things you don't want anymore.

Check your list, my dear. I hope you got the things you really wanted. If not, I hope you will.

The second letter will be delivered three weeks after the first. It will tell you to keep believing that good things can happen. Your hope may be wearing thin by then. I hope this second letter will make it thicker. If we're lucky, the second letter will reach you when you need it most.

The third letter is in your hand, obvs.

Beloved Emma, I want you to know that luck is not a thing that happens to you. Luck is *everything* that happens to you. The good, the bad, the in-between. And luck is what you make happen. Luck is how you see the events of your life, and how you respond to them.

I learned a lot from this stupid cancer. Mostly I learned that to be a soul in a body is the luckiest thing in the world. Imagine: out of all the people who were never born, we got to live! We were given a chance to experience life—to think, to love, to feel. My God, Emma, every day on earth is a complete miracle. I wish I'd known sooner how lucky we are to be alive.

I can't believe I'm going to miss out on all the lucky things that will happen for you in your life. And I wish I could be there for the bad things, too.

When painful things happen, you'll know that I am there with you in spirit. *Literally.*

Be good to yourself. And be good to your mom. And know that you were so, so good to me.

I love you,
Aunt Jenny

I finished reading the letter, and I pressed it to my chest. I wanted it to sink into my skin. Of course it was Aunt Jenny who brought magic into my life. She always had. I had the strongest sense of her presence—I heard her voice in my head, I saw her face in my mind, and I could feel her smiling at me as though she were right there in front of me.

Fran watched as I read the letter. She handed me a tissue. It almost looked like she could use one herself.

"Jenny was a very special person," she said. "I wouldn't have played messenger for anybody else."

"Thank you, Fran." I hugged her before she could stop me. She froze stiffly.

"Oh, for the love of Pete," she muttered. "You got your letter—now scram."

I ran upstairs with the letter. Mom was FaceTiming with Darren, but she stopped short when she saw my tear-strewn face. "Emma?"

I handed her the letter. She saw the handwriting and looked up at me, astonished. "What is this?" she asked, tears in her eyes. "When did this come? How did . . . ? I don't . . ."

"Read it," I said.

Mom began to weep. "I don't know if I can."

"Kate," Darren said gently via the laptop. "I'm going to let you go now. Call me later, or whenever you feel like it."

Mom nodded and ended the call.

I sat down at the table next to Mom and took her hand. She squeezed it hard. When I was a little kid and I had to get shots at the doctor, she used to let me squeeze her hand until it was purple. Now it was her turn to hold on to me.

"No," she said as she started to read. She put the letter down and cried. "No, no, no. Oh, Jenny. I can't."

"Mom," I said. "It's okay. It's good. It's really good."

Mom shook her head no. "It's too hard. I can't stand it. I can't stand that she's gone."

"I know," I said. I squeezed her hand this time. "But here she is."

Mom nodded through her tears. She collected herself, and bravely started reading. Almost instantly, she collapsed again and put the letter down.

"Keep going, Mom."

She tried again. And this time, she managed to keep reading. She cried and cried in big, hoarse gasps—at one point it almost sounded like she was laughing, she was crying so hard—but she kept reading. When she finished, she pressed the letter to her chest, just like I had. Then she looked up and spoke to the ceiling.

"I miss you so much, Jenny. I miss you so, so much. I wake up, and I can't believe you're gone. I feel like I'm missing a limb. You were in so much pain . . . I don't want to be selfish. But I wish you didn't have to go so soon. I wish you could have stayed . . ."

She was talking to Aunt Jenny like she was there in the kitchen with us. Just like I felt her, so did Mom. Mom talked and talked and cried and pounded her fist on the table and startled Penguin. I held on to her other hand.

And so we sat, crying and hugging and talking to Aunt Jenny. I told her all about the play, and Lewis, and how we saved Venice. Mom told her about Conrad the cad and Darren with the ex-girlfriend; about Brik and Derek, and Casey and her awful husband Ken, and all their mutual friends. We wept ourselves empty, until we were laughing again, thinking about all the good times we had together.

And I felt it all around me, strong as any physical force, sure as any miracle.

The impossible had happened. Aunt Jenny had come back, and she'd always be with us from now on.

Epilogue

IT'S JULY NOW, AND WE'RE HERE ON FIRE Island. We're at the bay where the horseshoe crabs live, waiting for sunset, when we'll let Aunt Jenny's ashes go.

I've thanked her for the letters so many times now. Each time, I know she's saying the same thing she always said, standing right here on this spit of sand as she pitched crabs back into the bay where they belonged. *Live your life to the fullest,* she says. *That's thanks enough for me.*

It's not just me and Mom and Penguin tonight. Darren's here, and he brought Lancelot, the three-legged dog he adopted from Waggytail.

Darren and Lancelot are living up at Herbie's brownstone while he dissolves the business he had with Pauline and looks for a job in New York. I like having him around, most of the time, except when he and Mom are being all crazy-in-love with each other, and I'm like, *Hi, this is awkward.*

But it's not like they can hide it. Everybody can see how happy Darren and Mom make each other. Mom's still sad from losing Aunt Jenny, but she's not lonely anymore. Tonight, as the still-shining sun turns the clouds rose gold, I hold one of Mom's hands while Darren holds the other.

(Then there's Grandma. While we're over here holding hands, she's struggling to keep Lancelot's and Penguin's leashes from tangling. They refuse to stop playing with each other, even though this is supposed to be a Serious Moment of Reflection. "These dogs need training," she mutters, but I know she adores them. As long as they don't bring sand into the house.)

The magic of Aunt Jenny's letters ended over a

month ago, but my good fortune kept coming. Melanie was able to explain to Ms. Engel what happened the day I missed rehearsal, and Ms. Engel grudgingly let me come back to play Nadine. Brooke, Geneva, and my other cast friends had extra rehearsals to help me catch up on what I missed. Then, five days before the play, the unthinkable happened: Jason, my leading man, was playing Ultimate Frisbee in the park, and he broke his leg.

"It's just an expression!" Ms. Engel yelled in front of the whole cast and crew. "You're not actually supposed to break your leg!"

Fortunately, Lewis's "dad" (older brother) was able to cancel their "trip to the Philippines," so Lewis was able to step in and play the role of Julian. And that's how I wound up *not* kissing the handsomest guy in school onstage in front of everyone. Twice.

The reviews, btw, were sensational, except for Carter forgetting one or two of his lines. "Sorry I blanked," he apologized afterward. "All I could think of was 'banana.'" And Lewis gave me two dozen origami roses as I took my bows. I don't know who took more teasing for it: me from Brooke and those guys, or Lewis from his (now former) friends. But I know who *doesn't care at all*: us.

Brooke's coming out to the beach when she gets back from drama camp—alone. Our little cast cluster hasn't been the same since Geneva and Harrison got together at the party after the show. (I KNOW.) Now they're a couple, and we're all still friends, but sometimes I feel like *I'm* at drama camp.

Vannah is visiting next weekend with her moms. She still doesn't have a real phone, or any online activity, but at least her moms are letting her out of the house again, and she's getting a fresh start at a magnet school for visual arts in the fall. We write each other letters now (hers are illustrated, mine have stick figures) at least twice a week, which is surprisingly fun. It's really gratifying to get an envelope with your name on it, even if it's not a lucky note with twenty bucks inside.

We even brought Herb and Jack with us to the beach. Mom finished scanning all their old photos, and she and Darren gave the originals and the film reels to the Fire Island Historical Society, which put them on exhibition at the community house for the summer. They made a four-foot poster of one photo to advertise the exhibit, so every time we pass the community house, we see Herb and Jack with their arms around each other's shoulders, smiling and waving hello.

And when Lewis gets back from visiting his grandparents, he'll come out for the day, and I'll show him how to rescue upside-down crabs with a shovel. We'll take a walk on the beach, we'll wave to Bobby Dudderman and his new girlfriend, Lacy, and I'll explain how the advent of plastic bottles led to a paucity of beach glass.

How lucky am I?

Acknowledgments

THANKS

Joy Peskin, Joy Peskin, Joy Peskin, Joy Peskin, Joy Peskin, Joy Peskin, Joy Peskin, Joy Peskin, Joy Peskin, Joy Peskin, Joy Peskin, Joy Peskin, Joy Peskin, Joy Peskin, Joy Peskin, Joy Peskin, Joy Peskin, Joy Peskin, Joy Peskin, Joy Peskin

ALSO THANKS

Nicholas Henderson

Aimee Fleck

Gene Hult

Erin Eisner, Isabelle Stern, Rachel Weiss, and Jonathan Yellen

Madison Cavone, Michael Cavone, Sofia DiGennaro, Julian Feign, Madison Forrest, Jill Frezza-Charbonier and her students, Gabriella Moncaleano, Gianna Perlman, Miles Perlman, Grace Rivkis, Gabe Safir, Simon Sinnreich, Vaughn Stout, and Trenton Wilson

Jill Abrahams, David Brouillard, Satia Cecil, Chris Donovan, Jen Dziura, Emilie Blythe McDonald, Bill and Laura Reynolds, Naomi Rivkis, Melissa Roth and Erik Seims, Tia Schellstede, Caitlin Schoenfeld, Kevin Scurry, and Anne Sussman

Dr. Robin Young

Larry and Sylvia Erlbaum

Bill Scurry

NO THANKS

Minky

Velvet

Waggytail Rescue is a real dog rescue organization based in New York City. Founded in 2004 by Holly DeRito, Waggytail is a registered 501(c)(3) non-profit that has found homes for over five thousand animals. A portion of the proceeds from this book have been donated to Waggytail so they can continue to rescue dogs. If you'd like to donate money, foster or adopt a dog, or volunteer, please visit waggytailrescue.org.